BLIND RIVER

A THRILLER

BEN FOLLOWS

For my Parents,
without your endless support this book would never have existed.

CHAPTER 1

"Someone better be dead," Curtis Mackley whispered as he opened the door.

His partner, FBI Agent Frankie Lassiter, stood a few feet back from the door, dressed as though she'd had hours to prepare. She was tall enough to block Curtis's view of the streetlights.

"That's such a dark way to start a conversation," she said. "I was worried your doorbell didn't work. I tried calling you, but your phone is off."

"Yeah, my sister kept calling me. Why are you here, Frankie? We don't need to be keeping track of that banker until seven."

Frankie shrugged. "Someone died."

Curtis perked up. "Someone died? We have a new assignment? Thank God. Where?"

"I don't know," said Frankie. "Johnson called and said we needed to be in the FBI offices by six. He said we should plan to be gone for at least a few days."

Curtis nodded. "I'll be out in a minute."

He shut the door. Inside, he brushed his teeth and climbed into the shower. It was only as the water ran over his body that he thought of the promise he'd made to Melanie. He cursed, then pushed it out of his head.

After his shower, he pulled on the only dry-cleaned suit he had and packed the others. He considered letting Melanie sleep, then thought better of it. He walked upstairs and shook her awake, breaking her out of a snore.

"Curtis?" She looked up at him. "What time is it?"

"Just before six," said Curtis. "Frankie is here. We have a case."

Melanie blinked a few times to clear away the sleep. She leaned over and turned on the light, then sat up against the headboard. She repositioned herself to more comfortably fit her growing stomach. "I thought you had that case in Manhattan. I thought you'd be here."

"This is a real case. We might be away for a few days. I'll be back as soon as I can. For you and the baby."

Melanie looked him in the eyes. "Come here."

"What?"

"Come here."

Curtis stepped closer. Melanie took his hand and moved it, so it was resting on her stomach. "This is your child," she said, holding his hand there. "Promise me you'll come back."

"This is different," said Curtis. "I never loved Amber like I love you."

"Promise me," said Melanie.

Curtis tried to remove his hand from Melanie's stomach, but her grip held firm. She looked at him with a doubt that hurt his soul, but he knew it was justified. He thought of

Amber, of the same moments with her. That child would be eight now. He didn't want to think of that.

"Curtis," said Melanie. "Promise me."

He nodded, bringing his focus back to the present. "I promise."

Melanie looked into his eyes for a few moments before letting go of his hand and forcing a smile. "Okay. Tell Frankie I said hi."

She turned away from Curtis and pulled the blankets over her. "Turn off the light on your way out."

Curtis did so, looking back at Melanie for a moment before leaving the room.

Within less than ten minutes he was outside, a travel mug of coffee held tight in his hand and his suitcase trailing him. He locked the door and checked it several times. He glanced around the house to make sure there were no open windows, nor easy access points.

"It's safe," said Frankie. "We'll be late if you keep locking stuff up."

Curtis nodded, tried the door once more, and followed Frankie to the car. He threw his luggage into the trunk and sat in the passenger seat.

At FBI HEADQUARTERS, Frankie and Curtis flashed their identifications to the gate agent and were waved inside. On the tenth floor, they walked through the bullpen of overworked FBI agents to Director Johnson's office.

They knocked on the door and heard, "Come in."

Director Johnson, a broad-shouldered black man with just enough white hair to make him look experienced without being out of touch was sitting behind his desk. Drawn blinds partially blocked the view of the Hudson River.

"Thanks for coming so early," said Johnson. "Take a seat."

"Someone better be dead," said Curtis as he took his seat.

Johnson let out a single laugh.

"Don't encourage him," said Frankie, taking her seat. "What have you got?"

"Well," said Johnson. "I'm sorry to disappoint you, Curtis, but we don't have a murder. At least, not for sure."

"What have you got?" said Frankie.

"Four young girls between the ages of seventeen and nineteen have disappeared from the same town. We need you to go out there and help the local police investigate."

"Good enough," said Curtis. "Where are we going?"

"I'm surprised you don't already know, Curtis," said Johnson. "I would have thought you'd heard about this."

Curtis shrugged. "I have no idea."

"You're going to Blind River. Your hometown."

"You're kidding me." Curtis looked back and forth between Frankie and Johnson, but neither gave any ground. "Are you fucking kidding me? Can we go back to monitoring the banker, please?"

"No, you can't," said Johnson. "We'll give the banker job to some of the incompetents who just graduated from the academy. This is your assignment. Deal with it. I'm shocked you hadn't heard about it. The request came from a police detective in Blind River named Monica Mackley. A relation of yours?"

Curtis tensed up. "That's my sister. She's been calling me a lot the last week. I haven't spoken to her in five years. I didn't know it was anything like that."

His hands clenched the thin metal arms of the chair. Frankie watched him, then turned to Johnson.

"Sir," said Frankie, "isn't this a conflict of interest? Curtis could be directly involved with suspects in the case."

Johnson nodded. "Curtis is a professional. I have faith in him. Detective Mackley didn't mention Curtis by name, but if she's calling him, that's probably who she was hoping for. We don't have any other agents with your skillsets who aren't on assignment. Besides, this is a small-town thing." Johnson checked his watch. "Your plane is scheduled to leave in about an hour. You should get going."

Frankie stood. After a moment Curtis did the same. They took the case files from Johnson and walked out of the office. Curtis paused in the door, trying to come up with a valid reason for dropping the case. He came up with nothing and walked after Frankie.

As the elevator descended, Curtis said, "This sucks."

Frankie looked at him. "What's so bad about Blind River? Why are you so nervous about going back there?"

Curtis didn't answer as the elevator arrived at the ground floor.

On the street, he asked Frankie to wait for him, then walked over to a mailbox. He took an unsealed envelope from his pocket. Inside was a wad of bills. He checked that there was the right amount and that the address on the front was correct.

Once he was sure, he sealed the envelope and slipped it into the mailbox. He turned and walked away, wondering whether the intended recipient would get the money.

He didn't even know if Amber still lived at that address.

CHAPTER 2

THE PLANE TOOK OFF FROM THE TARMAC OF THE PRIVATE airfield toward the rising sun. Curtis and Frankie were the only passengers on the hour-long flight to Blind River. Curtis had been concerned the plane would be too large to land on the Blind River airstrip but had been assured it was no issue. Frankie had looked at him like he was making excuses.

From the plane phone, paid for by the FBI, Curtis called Melanie.

"Hello?" she answered. There were sounds of commotion. Melanie was probably getting dressed to go to work. She still had two weeks at the advertising firm before her pregnancy leave began.

"Hey," said Curtis.

"Why are you calling?" said Melanie.

"Maybe I just wanted to call and talk."

"Curtis. You never call me just to talk. That's my job."

Curtis looked out the window at the passing clouds. "The case is in Blind River."

Melanie was silent for a long moment. She was the only

person who knew everything that had happened there. "Will it be alright?"

"I don't know. If Marino isn't involved in the case, it shouldn't matter."

Frankie looked up from the case files she was reading but said nothing.

"There's no shame in quitting the case," said Melanie. "I'm sure Johnson would understand."

"No," said Curtis, realizing he had never actually intended to drop the case. "I think it'll be good for me."

"Your family will be there."

Curtis sighed. "Monica is the one who was calling me."

"When was the last time you spoke to them?"

Curtis looked down at the wedding ring on his finger. "Before I met you."

"So they don't know?"

"No," he said, thinking of the ultrasound and the small heartbeat. "They don't."

"Are you going to tell them?"

"I don't know."

Melanie sighed. "It would be nice if you did."

"Melanie."

"I know. Just think about it, okay?"

"Okay."

Melanie sighed. "Call me if you need anything. I love you."

"I love you too."

The call ended, and Curtis lowered the phone.

Frankie, not looking away from the case file, said, "Going to call your sister?"

Curtis looked at the phone in his hand. "I'll see her when we get to Blind River."

"Call ahead," said Frankie. "Let her know you're coming, so it isn't such a huge shock when you meet face to face."

Curtis looked at the phone for a few moments before dialing the number.

"Detective Mackley," came the clipped answer. It made Curtis pause, his memories running wild of his younger sister, the person he had once sworn to protect at all costs and had then completely ignored.

"Hello?" said Monica. "Anyone there?"

"Hey, Monica," said Curtis.

There was a pause. "Curtis?"

"Yeah."

"Finally replying to my call?" said Monica. "It only took me calling the Federal Bureau of Investigation to get you to talk to your own sister?"

"I didn't know about the kidnappings. I would have answered if I had known."

"You would have answered if you had thought I wasn't just calling as a sister?"

"Do you want my help or not?" said Curtis.

"I really don't, honestly," said Monica. "I can solve this myself. I don't need your help, but the chief disagrees."

"Monica, I didn't—"

"Dad wants to see you."

Curtis didn't reply for a moment, the sudden change in topic throwing him off. "How is he?" he said.

Frankie squirmed in her seat.

"Not good," said Monica. "He misses you. He talks about you all the time."

"Tell him I'll see him when I get there."

"He wants you at dinner tonight."

"I might have to work on the case," said Curtis, "the first forty-eight hours—"

"They've been missing for weeks, Curtis. The first forty-eight hours don't matter for shit anymore. Maybe if you had answered my calls, but not anymore."

"Look, Monica," said Curtis, his voice rising as he spoke, "I didn't know about the case, and I wouldn't even be talking to you if I didn't, so give it a rest, okay?"

"Come to dinner, Curtis," said Monica. "He's your father. You owe him that much. It shouldn't take a bunch of girls getting kidnapped and possibly, probably, killed to get you to visit occasionally. I'll see you when you get here."

The line went dead. Curtis stared at the phone for a moment. Frankie crossed and uncrossed her legs a few times in his peripheral.

Curtis put the phone back into its cradle and walked through the plane to the small bathroom, where he splashed his face in the sink.

He took a few deep breaths, splashed his face a second time, checked himself in the mirror, and returned to his seat across from Frankie. He grabbed one of the case files and read through it as the plane began its descent toward Blind River.

CHAPTER 3

CURTIS WAS SURE THAT THE AIRSTRIP WAS TOO SHORT TO LAND on, but the pilot managed to land with distance to spare and come to a gentle stop.

They thanked the pilot and exited the plane, Frankie ducking through the door. The small airfield was mostly used by crop dusters and helicopters. The runway was cracked and uneven, and the hangars which dotted the airstrip were rusted and in disrepair.

Standing on the tarmac were two men and one woman. It took Curtis a few seconds to recognize the brunette woman wearing a black suit jacket and sunglasses was his sister. She stood with poise and confidence he hadn't seen before. She was about eight inches shorter than Frankie but emanated the same kind of authority.

The men looked like cardboard cutouts of the many police detectives and police chiefs Curtis had met. The man he assumed was Monica's partner was average height, but built like a stick. The other man had grey hair, his gut hanging out over his belt. Curtis didn't recognize either of the men, although he had barely recognized his own sister.

Curtis looked back at the plane before walking toward the welcome party.

Monica stepped forward.

"Thanks for coming," she said to Curtis, holding out a hand.

Curtis shook his sister's hand, feeling an odd distance.

"Good to see you again, Monica," he said.

"Good to see you, too, Curtis."

Frankie stepped in and held out a hand. "Special Agent Frankie Lassiter, nice to meet you."

"Detective Monica Mackley," said Monica. "This is my partner, Detective Trevor Marshall." She indicated the detective. "And this is Chief Frank Tucker." She indicated the other man. "Tucker was transferred in from another town a few years back, so Curtis won't remember him, but Trevor was in high school with us."

"Of course I remember Trevor," said Curtis. He shook Trevor's hand, not remembering him at all.

The others made their introductions.

"Let's get going," said Trevor. The chief stood a few steps behind him. "I'm sure you'll want to get up and running as soon as possible."

Curtis put his hands into his pockets. "How are we getting to the station?"

Trevor looked to the chief, who said, "You two will be riding with the detectives. My car doesn't have enough room unless you want to sit behind the grate. We'll get you set up with a car as soon as possible."

They walked out of the airfield and loaded their luggage

into the trunk of Monica and Trevor's car. The detectives climbed up front while Curtis and Frankie climbed into the back. As they left the airfield, the plane took off behind them.

"So, Curtis," said Trevor from the passenger seat, "you don't remember me at all?"

Curtis laughed. "Was I that obvious?"

"I'm a detective," said Trevor. "I'm not surprised. I was quiet and not very social in high school. I wouldn't remember me either."

"Don't mention it," said Curtis, not paying attention. He was looking out the window at the pine trees which lined the road leading into Blind River.

"Blind River," muttered Frankie. "Kind of a weird name. Where's it come from?"

An image of a pond deep in the forest which he and his friends had dubbed the "True Blind River" popped into Curtis's mind.

"There's a river, obviously," said Trevor. "A lot of early settlers came here because it was a good trade route, or at least they thought it was. The river has a turn where you're immediately at a waterfall. A lot of people died from rowing over it. Once they turned the corner, it was too late. So, the river was named the Blind River, and the town was built up around it."

"Interesting," said Frankie. "Population?"

"Around five thousand."

"Industry?"

"Funny you should ask. We'll be able to see it just about now."

The trees cleared away, and Curtis saw what he remembered and dreaded most about Blind River. On their left side, they could see a four-lane highway used primarily by transport trucks. The highway was always busy, but most of the traffic passed through on its way to somewhere else.

On the other side of the road was an immense gray building resembling a castle. The Blind River Maximum Security Penitentiary stretched into the sky. The grey walls and sentry outposts blocked the sun. The only people visible were the gate agents and guards with rifles standing on the walls, looking over the prison yard.

Monica glanced at the prison, watching Curtis's expression in the rearview mirror.

Trevor continued explaining the logistics of the prison to Frankie. He explained how it had single-handedly solved the economy of Blind River a decade back and how a large percentage of the population was working in the prison or in related industries.

The prison and the highway disappeared from view as they drove into downtown Blind River. It was nothing more than a short row of stores and offices which served as a center point of the spoke-and-wheel pattern the town was built on. The Presbyterian church stood in the center of the town.

Each of the stores and offices was one of a kind, with no competition. There was one butcher, one bookstore, one grocery store, all locally owned.

Cutting through the middle of the downtown was a river large enough for a medium sized boat. They crossed the bridge and Curtis looked down at the murky green water. The river was polluted, the bottom covered in beer bottles and garbage tossed off the bridge in the dead of night. There were signs prohibiting dumping in the river, but the police had long since given up trying to regulate it.

Despite the shining sun, they only passed six or seven cars on the way into town. The stores lining the main road were empty, with prominent "Sale" signs which seemed to beg for customers.

"Where is everyone?" said Curtis.

"Staying home," said Monica. "They're scared. Four girls have disappeared. Everyone knows or recognizes at least one of the girls. We need to make this town safe again before it starts falling apart."

They pulled into the police station and walked inside. The chief was waiting. They were instructed to leave their luggage in the car for the time being.

"Where are we staying?" said Frankie. "I saw a motel by the highway. We can get rooms there if it's needed."

"It's fully booked," said Monica. "We're working on accommodations. We'll let you know as soon as we do."

They walked through the small bullpen where the detectives had their desks. The station was mostly empty save for the receptionist and a few tired detectives. On the far side of the station was a door leading to a small jail. Trevor explained that it had four cells and that they were currently unoccupied.

Curtis and Frankie nodded to the other detectives in greeting and proceeded into a back room, which Trevor explained was their war room. A whiteboard had been set up along one wall to keep track of the investigation.

Four pictures of young girls were at the top of the board, and beneath those were lists of information about their disappearances. Curtis was shocked at how young they looked. According to the data beneath the pictures only one was out of high school.

"You've read the files we sent?" said Trevor as they took their seats around the conference table. Chief Tucker took a seat farther back, making it clear he was only there to observe.

"Yes," said Frankie, taking the lead as she always did. "For the sake of making sure we have all the information, assume we don't know anything. Start from the beginning."

Monica and Trevor took up spots on either side of the board. Curtis crossed his hands in his lap and lounged back in the swivel chair.

"Three weeks ago," began Monica, gesturing to the first picture, of a young girl with flowing blonde hair and too much makeup, "Ashley Hagerty, seventeen, didn't come home late at night. She'd been fighting with her parents, and they assumed she was at a friend's house. When she didn't show up at school the next day, her parents called the police. We figured she'd run away. It wasn't until the next ones started disappearing that we took it seriously."

"Five days later," said Trevor, taking over and pointing to a picture of a confident, athletic girl, "was the disappearance of Darcy Oberman, eighteen. She missed the bus to her volleyball game. No one thought anything had happened until later that day. The kidnapper had a ten-hour head start."

Trevor pointed to the map of Blind River in the middle of the board. There were four red tacks. He explained that each red tack was the home of one of the victims. The other colors represented the last known locations and places of interest. Curtis stared at the map, trying to see a pattern, but it all seemed random.

"The third disappearance happened ten days ago," said Monica. "Trevor and I put aside our other cases to focus on this." She pointed to the third picture, of a brown-haired, innocent looking girl with a butterfly clip in her hair. "Miranda O'Connell, eighteen, disappeared on her way back from piano lessons. She never made it home. Her parents called immediately. We found the butterfly clip near a local park." Trevor gestured to a picture of a mud-covered hairclip. "There is a park where the lights shut off around ten. She disappeared somewhere in that fifty-foot stretch."

"Then three days ago," said Trevor, "Harriet Matheson, seventeen, disappeared." Trevor gestured to the final picture, of a girl with a variety of piercings covering her face and pink and green streaks in her black hair. "She was out drinking with friends by the woods and left to buy more cigarettes. She never came back."

"We didn't find anything," said Monica. "The butterfly hairclip is the only piece of evidence we've recovered. It didn't have any fingerprints or DNA on it. We've interviewed everyone we can think of. We have stacks of investigation reports. I've learned more about the people in this town than I ever wanted to know. We have no suspects, no leads, and no answers."

"So," said Frankie, "we have four teenage girls from different cliques and friend groups who have been kidnapped and possibly killed while they were out at night in various parts of Blind River. Have you checked if any strange people have arrived in Blind River? Maybe a trucker who stops at the motel often?"

"Nothing we could find," said Monica.

Frankie nodded. "We'll double check, but let's assume for the time being that the murderer is a local. Curtis, we need to get to work. Monica, Trevor, set up a meeting with the rest of the police department in an hour. I'd like to talk to them all."

"Of course," said Trevor.

Curtis and Frankie stood and walked to the door.

"There is one other thing," said Monica.

Curtis and Frankie turned back.

"Someone in the police department is giving information to the local paper, The Blind River Observer," said Monica. "They know way too much about the case. Someone is talking to a reporter named Natasha Nolowinski."

"Natasha?" said Curtis. "I remember her. She was a bitch."

Trevor shot a look at Curtis.

"Well," said Monica, "she still is."

Curtis sighed. "We need a car."

"We can drive you," said Trevor.

"No," said Frankie. "We need to check out the crime scenes without any preconceived notions. A completely blank slate. Car?"

"You can use mine," said the chief, who Curtis had forgotten was sitting at the back of the room. "I'll be here all day anyway. Just make sure it's back by five. I'll get you set up with an actual car by tomorrow."

Frankie nodded.

"Wait," said Chief Tucker as they turned to leave. "Why did you say, murderer?"

"Because I'm an optimist, Chief," said Frankie. "If they're still alive, they're being put through things that no one should ever have to imagine, let alone experience. For their sake, I hope they're dead."

CHAPTER 4

CURTIS AND FRANKIE STARTED WITH THE MOST RECENT kidnapping. If they were going to find anything, it would be there. They both knew very well that once the crime scene was opened up, the chances of finding anything were essentially zero.

Normally, Frankie insisted on seeing the crime scenes, claiming it gave her a better visualization of the crimes. Curtis was perfectly happy looking at maps and pictures, a method which Frankie saw as impersonal. To Curtis, that was the point. The moment you lost your objectivity, you lost your ability to solve the case.

Curtis felt strange as they drove through town. It was the same town he'd grown up in, but it wasn't.

"This place is shittier than I remember," he muttered.

They found the spot at the edge of the woods where Harriet Matheson and her friends had been smoking and drinking. They parked the car in a lot at the edge of the dense forest.

There were beer bottles and cigarette butts on the ground. The footprints had been destroyed by rain two days prior. They only knew the spot from the maps they'd been given.

"What do you figure?" said Frankie, looking around.

Curtis crouched beside the beer bottles on the ground. He looked into the forest.

"Closest place to buy cigarettes would be the convenience store about half a mile back toward downtown," he said. "If I were the kidnapper, I'd wait in the forest, come out when Harriet was least expecting it, grab her around the mouth, drag her into the woods."

"You don't think he took her somewhere?" said Frankie.

Curtis shook his head. "I don't know why you'd do it so close to the forest if you didn't intend to use it as cover."

Frankie nodded. She took out her iPhone and began snapping pictures of the scene. Once she was finished, she said, "Let's walk up to the convenience store and talk to whoever's there. Maybe that can give us some idea."

"I don't see how this fits in with the other kidnappings," said Curtis. "All the others were downtown or in the residential areas."

Frankie shrugged. "It has to be one guy. The chances of multiple kidnappers attacking the same kind of victim in the same town, which hasn't had anything like this for two decades, is too low to even think about. He's probably trying to be unpredictable."

"What about one main guy and one copycat?"

"It's possible," said Frankie, "but copycats are normally terrible. They get caught and confess. They're weak and stupid. We'd have more evidence to work with."

Curtis stood and began walking in the direction of the convenience store. Frankie followed closely.

"We assume it's one person for the time being," said Curtis, "and that it's probably a local, but we'll check that."

"It might be someone you know," said Frankie.

"Yes," said Curtis. The name "Marino" jumped into his head, even though he knew it was impossible. "It could be."

Curtis looked up at the prison in the distance.

"So," said Frankie, "what's the deal with you and Monica? Seems like there's some bad blood there?"

Curtis shrugged. "Just sibling stuff."

He looked over the lake. He realized Frankie wasn't with him and looked back.

She had stopped. She was standing at the edge of the water, gazing at the far side of Lake Ontario, the faint silhouette of Toronto in the distance.

"What are you looking at?" said Curtis.

"What did you think of Trevor Marshall?" said Frankie.

"I think he's a good detective. He seems to know what he's doing."

"And the chief?"

"I would have preferred someone I know, but he seems to be good at his job."

Frankie paused for a moment. "You need to tell me what's going on, Curtis. What are you so afraid of?"

Curtis jerked his head toward her. "What are you talking about?"

"You're distracted. None of these people have dealt with anything like this before. Chief Tucker might be a good man, but he's not a good cop, or else he wouldn't be here. You're not noticing things like you usually do."

"It's nothing," said Curtis. "I'll be fine."

"You're looking at the prison again."

"What?" Curtis looked away from the prison, trying to play it off.

"Look, Curtis," said Frankie, "if you don't want to feel weak, that's fine. Tell me for my sake. You're my partner. If you're compromised, I'm being left out to dry in a town with a potential serial killer. I can't solve the case by myself."

"Yes, you could," said Curtis. "You're the best agent I've ever worked with."

"Don't ruin my point, Curtis. I need to know what's going on, especially if it's related to the case."

Curtis looked toward town, where the river the town was named after began. "You can't tell anyone what I'm going to tell you. Even if it's involved in the case."

"Okay."

Curtis took a deep breath. "How much do you know about the history of Blind River?"

"Almost nothing," said Frankie. "I had time to read the case file on the way here. I looked up the town on Wikipedia, but the article was only a dozen or so lines."

"The foundation of the town doesn't matter as much as what has happened in the last twenty years," said Curtis. "A major part of the Blind River economy was involved in the transportation of cocaine and methamphetamines."

CHAPTER 5

FRANKIE RAISED AN EYEBROW. "BLIND RIVER WAS INVOLVED IN the drug trade?"

Curtis looked at the ground for a moment, then looked up. "Some of the big drug lords of the south would use transport trucks to move their product. For example, if you're shipping furniture, put a few pounds of cocaine in the cushions. The cops started setting up roadblocks to check the trucks out on the highway. A local business owner named Sam Marino saw an opportunity. He made deals with the truckers to hide the product in his store and meet them on the other side of the roadblock."

Frankie nodded. "Who was chief at this time?"

"My dad, Chief Gordon Mackley."

"I didn't know your dad was a cop," said Frankie. "What did he think of all this?"

"He didn't know." Curtis paused and took a breath. "The truckers got used to using Marino as a workaround. They didn't mind if the product didn't add up perfectly. Marino started selling it out of his butcher shop. Then the truckers began giving him product in exchange for a percentage of profits. Everyone but the authorities seemed to know what was happening. Marino built it up to the point where he was manufacturing and distributing to a large section of the northeast United States. Within five years, almost everyone in Blind River was either involved with Marino or knew someone who was. It made getting anyone to testify impossible."

Frankie nodded. "No matter how bad someone was, whether they were a murderer, rapist or child molester, there will be someone at their funeral singing their praises."

Curtis nodded and continued. "When the police became aware of it, it was too late. No one would talk. Marino used his shop to launder his money. No one was falling for it, but it didn't matter."

"Why didn't they call the feds?" said Frankie.

Curtis shrugged. "The feds didn't care. We wouldn't even be here if there wasn't this weird lack of murders the last few weeks."

"Is Marino in prison?" said Frankie.

Curtis nodded.

"How'd that happen?"

"I'm getting to that." Curtis looked over the lake and took a deep breath. "I put him there."

Frankie frowned. "Weren't you like ten years old?"

"Twelve. I was working as a paperboy. Every morning I would deliver the New York Times and the Blind River Observer to Marino's shop. I got close to the people there. I would even get to hand deliver it to Marino. While I was coming and going, I would hear snippets of conversation. It didn't matter that I was the Chief's kid. They thought they were untouchable. I started wearing a recorder beneath my shirt, tucked into my pants. Over the next few months, I gathered enough information to make a case. I took the tapes to a lieutenant named Gerald Condra. He used the tapes, without revealing where he'd gotten them, to get warrants. In less than a year the town was cleared out. Marino and his inner circle were shipped off to prison."

"Who knows it was you?" said Frankie.

"Director Johnson knows," said Curtis. "I spoke to him about it before I started working at the FBI. Condra died about ten years ago in a car accident, so he's out. The judge of the case must know. If anyone found out, I could be in trouble. A lot of people in Blind River were working for Marino and lost their livelihoods because of the arrest. If not for the prison, Blind River would be broke."

"Marino is in the Blind River prison?"

Curtis nodded. "Once the prison was built, he requested a transfer so his family could visit. He must know it was me. He's had twenty years to think it over."

Frankie put her hands into her pockets. "Does your father know? Will that be a problem?"

Curtis nodded. "He's getting old. His mind isn't all there. If he knows, I'm worried he might slip and tell someone it was me."

"Thank you for telling me," said Frankie. "I appreciate it. We're a team. Never forget that."

Curtis checked his watch. "We'll need to be back at the station soon."

He turned to leave.

Frankie said, "Why don't we go to dinner tonight with

your sister and your dad? We can try to get a gauge on his mental health and whether or not he knows."

Curtis hesitated, then nodded. "That's a good idea. This whole walk was just a ruse for you to go all Oprah on me, wasn't it?"

Frankie smiled. "Guilty as charged."

CHAPTER 6

THEY WALKED ALONG THE HIGHWAY TOWARD THE CONVENIENCE store. They kept their eyes on the ground, looking for any clues that would indicate where the abduction had taken place. They found nothing and made it to the convenience store with twenty-five minutes left until they were due to be back at the station.

The convenience store was connected to a gas station Curtis didn't remember.

They walked inside. Curtis nodded to the man behind the counter.

"You the FBI fellows?" said the man, taking his feet off the counter and putting down his Playboy magazine. "I heard you were coming through town."

"Yeah," said Curtis, browsing the store. He walked up to the counter. "Special Agent Curtis Mackley. This is Special Agent Frankie Lassiter."

The man said, "I'm Hank."

"You know the girl who disappeared near here?"

"Sure, I know Harriet. I guess I should say that I knew Harriet, huh? Not much of a chance, is there?"

Curtis shrugged. "We aren't ruling anything out yet. What can you tell me about Harriet?"

"I didn't know her too well," said Hank. "She wasn't old enough to buy liquor and cigarettes, and I wasn't about to get my license revoked. Don't give me that look. It's true. I never sold to anyone who was underage. I take that shit seriously. Nothing I could do about Harriet's sister, though. I think she was coming in and buying Harriet whatever she wanted. Liquor, cigarettes, lottery tickets, you name it. Kendra, I believe her sister's name was. I think it would be worth your time to check her out."

Frankie scribbled notes onto her pad. "Did you see Harriet on the night she disappeared?"

"I already told all this to the cops," said Hank. "You can read their records."

"We like to do our own investigating," said Frankie. "We want to make sure they didn't miss anything. There are a lot of details people miss if they're inexperienced."

"Sure, I get that," said Hank. "Want something done right, you do it yourself. I didn't see Harriet on the night she disappeared. It was a slow night. There were only a few customers and only two who actually came in instead of paying with a card at the pumps. Harriet wasn't one of them. When I heard she'd disappeared, I went through all my security tapes from that night, trying to see if I'd caught anything. She was the fourth disappearance, so I was on edge. I didn't find anything."

"We'd like to get our hands on those tapes."

Hank nodded. "I can get those for you. Just for the night of the disappearance?"

"The twenty-four hours around it as well," said Frankie. "Noon the day before to noon the day after."

Hank looked skeptical for a moment, then took his feet off the counter and walked toward the back of the store. He came back about ten minutes later with eight disks, which each contained three hours of footage.

"Thanks," said Curtis, taking the disks. "We'll copy them and get them back to you as soon as possible."

Hank nodded, looking past them at the cars pulling up at the gas tanks.

"Can I get a pack of gum?" said Curtis, grabbing a pack and putting it on the counter.

Hank rang up the price, then waved his hand. "On second thought," he said, "take it for free. You're protecting our town. First time anyone from the federal government has cared about what happens here in almost two decades. Go catch the motherfucker who's taking those girls."

"Thanks for your help." Curtis raised the pack of gum in salute and walked out of the convenience store with Frankie in tow.

"He didn't recognize your name," said Frankie.

"I noticed," said Curtis. "It'll get out sooner or later."

They turned and retraced their steps along the shore. It was the same path the police must have walked endlessly, searching for clues as to what had happened to Harriet.

"How are you and Will doing?" said Curtis just as their car came into view.

Frankie looked up at him. "Why do you ask?"

"Like you said, we're partners. It helps me work the case if I know more about you. I haven't seen Will in a while."

"That's by intention," said Frankie sternly.

"How is he, though?"

"He's fine. He's working a lot."

"Still working at the same training facility?"

"Yeah," said Frankie, her tone indicating that the conversation was over.

Frankie and Will had met at the FBI academy. Both had been near the top of the class. They married on the night after they passed their final test. Frankie had continued her greatness out in the field. Will, on the other hand, had a nervous breakdown the first time he came face to face with a real criminal. He froze up and didn't react as the attacker ran toward him, knife raised in the air.

Will had just kept screaming, "Get back! Get back!"

He only survived because his partner, a twenty-year veteran of the Bureau, had shown up at the last second and put a bullet into the attacker's spine. Will had gotten out without any physical damage, but there had been no argument he should be taken out of the field. He had never attempted to prove them wrong and had settled into a cozy, safe job at the academy.

He and Frankie were still married, but his failure was considered a point of embarrassment for Frankie, who avoided the conversation whenever possible.

They got to their car and drove to the station.

Patrol cars filled the parking lot.

Curtis and Frankie parked in an empty spot and walked inside. The conversation quieted as the gathered officers saw them. Near the back of the packed room, Chief Tucker spoke with Monica and Trevor, shooting nervous glances toward the agents as they entered.

Curtis looked around the room and tried to pick anyone out he recognized. Although there was passing familiarity here and there, as though he had passed them on the street but never known their names, he recognized few. Curtis saw the same confused look being returned by the crowd.

"Everyone," said Chief Tucker, addressing the crowd, "these two FBI agents are here to help us investigate the disappearances. I'd like to introduce Special Agents, Frankie Lassiter, and Curtis Mackley. Some of you may know Curtis as the brother of Detective Mackley and the son of my predecessor, Chief Gordon Mackley. I'd like to thank them for taking the time to come assist us. Please give them your full attention."

Curtis felt the gazes of fifty police officers as they figured out why they recognized him. He hesitated for a moment, wondering if Frankie would overcome her fear of public speaking. She stood rigidly still and shot him a sideways glance. Curtis took the signal and stepped forward.

"Thank you, Chief Tucker, for the introduction," he said. "I'm FBI Special Agent Curtis Mackley. I lived in Blind River for the first eighteen years of my life. It's different from the last time I was here, but it's also remarkably similar. Some of you I recognize, some I don't, but throughout this investigation, we'll get to know many of you. My partner is FBI Special Agent Frankie Lassiter, and she is the smartest and most skilled person I've ever had the pleasure of working with."

The gaze of the crowd fell on Frankie. She raised one hand in an awkward wave, then looked at Curtis. He had never understood how she could talk down a serial killer with no problem, but the moment she had a group of people listening to her, she became scared and anxious.

"What's happened is a tragedy," Curtis continued, "and I wish I had a better reason to return to Blind River. Over the next few days, Agent Lassiter and I will be going through the case. The FBI will be setting up an anonymous phone line dedicated to this case. If you see anything suspicious, call that line. Later today, Agent Lassiter and I will be speaking at the school to make sure everyone is staying safe." Curtis glanced at Chief Tucker, who nodded his understanding that he would set up a speaking engagement at the school. "Any questions?"

A man Curtis vaguely recognized raised a hand and said, "What are the chances they're alive?"

Curtis looked at the man. "What's your name?"

"Joe Hagerty."

"Are you related to Ashley Hagerty?" Curtis said, remembering the name of the first girl who disappeared.

"She's my niece."

"I don't know if they're alive," said Curtis after a pause. He decided to be honest and tell the man what he needed to hear. "However, I wouldn't hold out hope."

Joe nodded, maintaining his composure, as though he'd already known the answer.

There were a few more questions which Curtis answered in short sentences, mostly due to his still shaky understanding of the case.

When all the questions were answered, Curtis said, "If anyone else wants to speak with us, don't hesitate. We're here to help, but this is your town. Hagerty, we'd like to speak with you and anyone else directly related to the victims. Thank you."

There was a scattering of polite applause, and the patrol officers dispersed, returning to their cars and driving off.

Joe and another officer approached. The other officer was young, thin and fit. He walked with the confidence of someone used to getting his way.

"This is Officer Matt Oberman," said Hagerty. "He's Darcy Oberman's brother."

Frankie took over. Now that it was only two people, her confidence had returned. "I'm sure this has been difficult for both of you."

"Thank you," said Matt. "I just hope Darcy's okay."

"We all do," said Frankie. "The reason we asked to speak with you is that we need to re-interview the families of the victims. It would be beneficial if we had someone with us who knew what they were going through."

"I don't know about that," said Matt. "My mum's already been through so much. My dad was never around, and if Darcy's gone, I'm all she's got. I think it might be too hard on her."

"Matt," said Frankie sternly. "If you want us to find your sister, we need to speak with your mother."

Matt nodded but avoided eye contact.

"What about you?" said Frankie, turning to Joe. "Can we speak to your family about it?"

Joe nodded. "I think so. My brother and his wife have been pretty distraught since their daughter vanished, but they'll want to help."

"Good," said Frankie. "Let's get going. We'll go in the car the chief loaned to us."

"Now?" said Matt. "My mum won't know we're coming. I don't think she can handle it."

"Yes, now," said Frankie. "Every moment we wait is another moment where Darcy, Ashley and the other girls could be dead or worse. Understand?"

Matt nodded. Joe looked like he was going to be sick.

"Wait here," said Curtis, seeing the chief waving to him from the office.

Curtis walked across the bullpen, weaving through the whispering officers. He stepped inside Chief Tucker's office, which was minimalist to an extreme. The only decoration was the chief's medal of commendation for bravery hanging on the walls. The bookshelves were piled high with books on crime and law, and the desk looked aged and weathered. Curtis wondered if his father had bought that desk.

"You wanted to see me?" said Curtis, taking a seat.

"Yes," said the chief. "Great speech out there. I just wanted to be clear as to what you wanted us doing here. I'll set up a time for you to speak at the high school."

"Within the next day if possible," said Curtis.

Tucker nodded. "Okay. It seems as though you've got things sorted out. What would you like the detectives working on?"

"I want records of everyone who has spent time in the prison or stayed at the Blind River Motel. I want dates, criminal records, and lists of any known acquaintances."

"Going back how far?" said Tucker.

"Six months."

Tucker nodded. "Anything else?"

Curtis took the disks from his pocket. "These are from the convenience store near where Harriet Matheson disappeared. Watch them closely. There might be something there."

"We already did that."

"Do it again."

Chief Tucker looked like he was about to argue, then thought better of it. "It'll be done."

"One other thing," said Curtis. "Sam Marino is in the prison out there, right?"

Tucker shifted in his seat. "He's there. I forgot you would have been here for all that shit. When I took over as chief, I was told it was a small prison town. It wasn't until I got here that someone took the liberty of filling me in. This was before the internet. I couldn't just Google that shit."

"Is there any chance this is related?" said Curtis.

Tucker shrugged. "It's possible, but I don't see how. We checked. Marino has made no escape attempts, no suspicious calls, and hasn't even stepped out of line. By all accounts, he's a model prisoner."

"Is that unusual?"

"Not according to the guards I've spoken to. Did you know those guys? Marino and them?"

Curtis stood and walked, hesitating in the doorway. "Yeah, I did."

"Is that why you became an FBI agent?"

Curtis just smirked and left the office, walking past the conference room where Monica and Trevor were sitting. Curtis leaned in the door and told them he and Frankie were heading out.

"What do you mean?" said Trevor, standing from his seat and sending the rolling chair backward. "This is our case. You can't just come in here and kick us off it like we're second rate helpers. We know what we're doing."

"Trevor," said Monica, holding out a hand. "What is it, Curtis?"

"I need you two to go through prison records and motel records over the last six months. Trevor, I understand, but we need to interview the families without any preconceived notions and be completely objective."

Trevor stared at him and said nothing.

"Will you be at dinner tonight?" said Monica, speaking calmly, as though she was trying to defuse the situation.

"Yeah," said Curtis curtly. "I'll be there. Frankie, too."

"We'll see you there."

Curtis nodded to Trevor before he left the room. As he walked away, he heard Trevor mutter, "Fuckin' FBI agent. Thinks he's so fucking special just because he got lucky. Prick."

CHAPTER 7

THE DRIVE TO THE HAGERTY HOME WAS DONE IN SILENCE.

They parked in front of the small, beige house. A white fence boxed in the back yard, and the tiles on the roof were fresher than the rest of the house, as though it was midway through a renovation. Joe took the lead as they walked up to his brother's front door. He knocked and waited.

Sounds of shuffling came from inside. After a minute, the door opened. An older woman wearing a bathrobe and slippers over her nightgown stood in the doorway. Her hair was a mess, as though she hadn't showered in days.

"Yes?" she said.

"Miriam," said Joe. "These two FBI agents have come to help find Ashley. They'd like to talk to you."

"I already spoke with the police," said Miriam to her brother-in-law, speaking in a monotone. "They haven't found anything."

"They're better than the police."

Miriam stared out vacantly. "I'm not dressed for it."

"It doesn't matter," said Joe. "Miri, come on. They can find Ashley."

Miriam nodded. "Come in. Would you like some tea?"

She turned and walked inside without waiting for their responses. The interior of the house was decorated with flower wallpaper and religious iconography. Joe indicated the living room, where a large painting of Jesus on the cross hung above the fireplace, and then went to find Miriam.

"Ken!" Miriam shouted from the kitchen. "Your brother brought the FBI!"

"Who?" came a groggy shout from upstairs.

"FBI!"

"Government pieces of shit!"

Curtis, Frankie, and Matt took their seats on the couch around the table. The sounds of someone rolling out of bed and stomping down the stairs echoed through the house. Joe and Miriam came into the living room. Joe placed a tray of tea and biscuits on the table.

Miriam looked as though she hadn't slept in weeks, probably since her daughter had disappeared. She fell into her recliner and looked at them over the table. "You're with the government?"

"The FBI," said Curtis.

The stomping came down the hall, and a man with a thick mustache hanging over his upper lip came through the door. He looked as though he was already drunk at 2:30 in the afternoon. He used the door frame to support himself.

Joe got up and led his brother across the room to an empty chair beside Miriam. Joe put out a hand, and his sister-in-law held it.

Miriam's husband, Ken, said, "So, you fellows are from

the government, huh? Think you're so fucking special that you can come out here and do a better job at finding my daughter than people who actually know this town? Fucking fair-weather cops is what you are. You just swoop in and take all the credit from the locals, just like the government always does. The working class does all the work, and the government and their banker buddies just come in and take all the money. This fucking country used to stand for something."

"Ken," said Curtis calmly, "I'd like you to know that I actually am a local. I spent the first eighteen years of my life in Blind River."

Ken frowned, as though he'd been thrown an unexpected curve ball. "What's your name, boy?"

"Curtis Mackley."

"You're Chief Mackley's boy? What a fucking hoot." Ken laughed. "So you're not just a government lackey, but you're selling out your own town. What a load of bullshit that is."

"Ken," said Curtis. "I need you to understand that Agent Lassiter and I are trained to deal with situations like this. But you're right. We don't know the town, and this isn't the town I knew as a kid. That's why we need your help. We need you to tell us everything about your daughter's disappearance."

"Fucking government cronies," mumbled Ken, but he seemed to have lost his energy. "Ashley deserves better than this bullshit. Two fucking agents is all they send."

"Ken," said Frankie. She indicated Joe and Matt. "These two officers both know what you're going through, and if you have any issues with what we do, I want you to speak with them, okay?"

Ken mumbled, "I guess you can't be any worse than these

incompetent fucks who work at the police station. What do you want to know?"

Frankie leaned in. "Tell us about Ashley. We need to know everything we can about her. Anything could be a clue."

"She was perfect." Ken looked to one side, as though looking for a memory in the wallpaper. "She was popular, she was smart, she was funny. I've never met anyone who didn't like her. I can't imagine anyone who would hurt her."

"No one? Not an ex-boyfriend or someone at school who didn't like her?"

Ken shook his head. "She wasn't allowed to have a boyfriend. It's too young for kids to be dating in high school. Miriam and I didn't date until we were in college. It's too young."

"What about enemies?"

Ken looked at Frankie as though she was crazy. "No, everyone liked her."

"After-school activities?"

"She was involved with the school paper, I think."

"Yes," said Miriam. "She was training to be a journalist. She was so talented and skilled."

"We've been trying to get her more involved with the church," said Ken, turning back to Frankie, "but she hasn't been going more than once a week. She'll come around."

Miriam let out a wail, and Joe squeezed her hand. Matt stood in the doorway, looking uncomfortable.

"Mr. Hagerty," said Frankie. "Do you mind if we see Ashley's room? Just to get a sense of who she is?"

Ken thought for a moment, then nodded. He stood slowly

and walked past them. Frankie and Curtis walked after him, up the stairs to the second story.

Ken opened the first door on the right and held it open for them. The roof of the bedroom was slanted. The decorations inside were a collection of Ashley's interests throughout her life. Barbies co-existed with Twilight novels and Bob Marley posters. The bed wasn't made. A half-eaten bag of chips and a can of Diet Coke sat on the bedside table. A series of fashion magazines were open on her desk.

Frankie walked to her closet and revealed a large wardrobe. It was much cleaner and well organized than the rest of the room. Frankie went through the clothing, looking for anything out of the ordinary.

Curtis stood a few feet back. He turned to the others. "Tell me about the night she disappeared," he said.

Miriam, standing just outside the room, let out another wail. "It's my fault," she said. "We were having a fight. I should have just let her do what she wanted."

"What happened?" said Curtis.

Ken answered, watching Frankie like a hound as she went through his daughter's clothes. "They were having a fight," he said. "Ashley didn't want to get involved at the church. She said she hates the people there. We thought it was regular teenager stuff. She didn't come home that night, but we didn't think anything of it. We thought she was at a friend's house."

"But she wasn't?"

Ken sighed. "No one saw her after that."

"Is there anything else we should know?"

"Not that I can think of."

Curtis nodded. "Frankie, you done?"

Frankie nodded, retreating from the closet. "I'm done."

They shook hands with the Hagertys and left the house. As they got to the door, Ken cleared his throat. Miriam stood behind him, refusing to let go of Joe's hand as he left. Matt was already out the door.

"Thank you," said Ken. "For what you're doing to find Ashley. I was angry earlier."

"We'll do our best to find her," said Frankie. "We promise."

"Thank you."

Joe wrestled his hand out of Miriam's and gave his sister-in-law a quick hug before following them. The screen door slammed shut behind them. Curtis wiped the sweat off his forehead as they walked to the car. Just as Curtis opened the passenger door of the car, a bright white flash caught Curtis from the right side. He clenched his eyes shut and threw his arms up.

CHAPTER 8

"AGENTS! SO NICE TO MEET YOU," SAID A FEMALE VOICE.

Curtis blinked to clear his eyes. He looked at the woman who had taken the picture. She held the camera in front of her chest. She had black hair pulled into a ponytail and a brown leather jacket. A notepad was jammed into her inside jacket pocket. The officers ignored her and climbed into the back seat.

"Natasha Nolowinski," said the woman, holding out a hand. "I'm a reporter with the Blind River Observer. Can I get a statement on your involvement in the search for the Blind River Killer?"

"No," said Curtis, climbing into the passenger seat. "If you want a statement, we'll be speaking at the school."

"Is it true there are no suspects?" said Natasha.

Curtis closed the door. "No comment."

"How does this relate to your sister, Agent Mackley? Did she call you in?"

Curtis turned to Frankie. "Drive."

Natasha leaned in the window. "What do you have to say about rumors that Sam Marino is involved?"

"Stop," said Curtis just as Frankie put the car into gear. He looked up at Natasha's smirk. "Where the hell did you hear that?"

"I can't reveal my sources," said Natasha. "Journalistic ethics."

"We're the FBI. I can arrest you for impeding an investigation."

"Oh," said Natasha, scribbling on her notepad. "Threatening a reporter about her free speech rights. That'll make an interesting story in tomorrow's paper."

"Forget it," said Curtis. "You don't know anything."

"Give me an interview, and I'll tell you more about Sam Marino."

Curtis rolled up the window and told Frankie to drive. He looked into the rearview mirror at the two officers. They both looked uncomfortable and awkward, but not guilty, so he mentally discounted them as being the leak, at least for the time being.

"Joe, Matt," said Curtis as they drove to Matt Oberman's house, "What do you think about the information being leaked?"

Joe let out a sound of disgust. "I think Natasha's a manipulative bitch, that's what I think."

"Any idea who could be leaking information?"

They both looked like they were about to say something, then responded with shrugs. Curtis knew no police officer would rat out one of his fellow officers, but it was worth the try.

"Maybe one of the family members is giving her information," said Matt. "Most of them are being kept up to date on the investigation."

"It's possible," said Curtis, not believing for a second that a family member had done it.

CHAPTER 9

THEY PULLED INTO THE DRIVEWAY OF A RED BRICK VICTORIAN house with a large yard.

Matt took the lead and knocked on the door. There was some shuffling inside. Curtis wondered if being unable to lift your feet was a symptom of a family member disappearing.

The door was answered by a woman who looked too young to be Matt's mother. She looked to be in her late thirties, with blonde hair and a fit body.

"Hey, Mom," said Matt, stepping up to the woman who looked more like his sister than his mother. He hugged her.

She hugged him back, looking over her son's shoulder at the others.

Matt pulled back. "Mom, these FBI agents want to talk about Darcy. They can help find her."

She looked at Curtis and Frankie for a moment before nodding. "I'm Kelly. Come in."

They were led into the living room and took their seats while Kelly disappeared for a minute.

While she was gone, Curtis walked over to the cabinet

beside the fireplace. It was filled with sports trophies from soccer and volleyball with a few thrown in from field hockey, from the local to the state level, almost all of which were awarded to Kelly Oberman. A few were awarded to Darcy Oberman, and fewer were awarded to Matt Oberman. He moved over to the mantle, looking through the photographs set up there. Nowhere in any of the photographs was there a man with Kelly. There was never anyone but her and the two kids.

Kelly returned a few minutes later with fresh clothing. She took her seat and cradled a cup of tea between her hands.

"You were quite an athlete," said Curtis, turning toward her. "Darcy follows in your footsteps."

"You think she's still alive?" said Kelly.

The hope in her voice almost broke Curtis then and there. "If she is," he said. "We'll find her."

Kelly nodded. "What do you need to know?"

"Anything about Darcy that might be connected to her disappearance. When was the last time you saw her? Anything like that."

"The last time I saw her?" Kelly paused for a moment. "It would have been at volleyball practice. I coach the high school team."

"Have you coached there for a long time?"

"About ten years now." Kelly was getting more comfortable, talking about her own accomplishments instead of her daughter's disappearance. "I was the captain of the volleyball and soccer team for two years, and when I got my teaching degree, they agreed to take me back. I've been teaching gym there for a while now." She reached to the side table and grabbed a carton of cigarettes. "Mind if I smoke?"

"No," said Curtis, although he tensed his nostrils as she lit the cigarette and opened a window to blow the smoke out. Frankie glanced at the cigarette with a look of disdain but said nothing. She had quit smoking two years earlier after three years of trying.

Kelly took a deep inhale on her cigarette and blew it out the window. Matt sat beside her, trying to look relaxed but constantly glancing at his mother, who still seemed far too young. Joe Hagerty stood in the doorway, looking uncomfortable, but having the decency to not check his phone or make an excuse to leave.

"I tried to keep my work and home life separate," said Kelly after a few moments, locking Curtis in her gaze as she spoke. "I never wanted Darcy nor Matt to feel like their mother was following them everywhere. I wanted them to have their own lives. If they chose to try out for my teams, that was their choice, and I would do everything in my power to treat them just like anyone else. Not that it mattered with Darcy. She's the best volleyball player I've ever seen. I can see her going to nationals in a few years."

Kelly crushed the cigarette into an ashtray on the side table and took another out of the packet. "Sometimes, I wonder if maybe I had been more of a controlling mother, if I had forced my will on her like I've seen other mothers do, maybe she would still be here."

Frankie said, "You can't think like that."

"I've read the self-help books," said Kelly. "I know I can't blame myself. I even spoke to the old chief about it. You probably won't know this, but the old chief had a kid who disappeared about fifteen years ago. Never found the kid. Old Gordon isn't too clear of mind, but he was still a huge help to me."

Curtis stood abruptly and walked out of the room, muttering an apology.

He walked onto the front porch and looked at the sunset. The sun was barely peeking through the dark storm clouds. He took a deep breath and wiped the sweat off his face.

"I hate this fucking town."

CHAPTER 10

CURTIS STARED ACROSS THE STREET THEN LOOKED BACK AT the house.

"What the hell was that about?" said Frankie. She closed the door behind her and stepped onto the porch.

To a casual observer, Frankie looked calm and collected, but Curtis knew her too well. There was anger and frustration brewing just beneath the surface.

Frankie stopped a few inches from Curtis's face. "What the hell is she talking about, Curtis? Your dad had a kid who disappeared? You never thought that was something you should bring up? Why the fuck are we even on this case? As soon as we're done here, you're telling me everything about this sibling who disappeared, and then we're calling Johnson and getting someone else sent out here."

Curtis shook his head. "I'll be fine. Don't call Johnson. I can't go back to the academy."

"You didn't look fine when you just scurried out of the house like a scared mouse. Why'd you do that? To get some fresh air, or to get away from talking about something you should have told me?"

"I'll tell you everything," said Curtis. "Just don't call Johnson. I can handle this."

Frankie stared at him for a moment. "You get one more chance. I'll finish the interview. We'll meet up later. We probably won't be able to do the last two families today anyway."

"I can suck it up," said Curtis, taking a deep breath. "We need to find out everything we can about these girls. What if they're still alive?"

Frankie shrugged. "The police have been looking. We have nothing to go on. We'll be better equipped to find them if we get a fresh start in the morning. If they're alive, we'll find them."

Curtis nodded but kept glancing back at the house.

"Get your mind off this," said Frankie. "I want to hear about this sibling of yours, and if I find out there is anything else that you haven't told me, literally anything, I'll be calling Johnson and getting you kicked out of the FBI, not just sent back to the academy. Do you understand me?"

"Understood." Curtis thought for a moment, remembering the luggage which was still in Monica and Trevor's detective car. "There's a bar downtown," he said, "called Randall's Tavern. I'll be there."

Frankie raised an eyebrow.

"I'll just have one or two beers," said Curtis. "I'll be fine for dinner at my dad's. I'll see you there."

"I'll get Joe to drive you."

"I don't need to be driven."

"It's not for you," said Frankie. "Joe looks like a kid who

needs to pee in church. Let him drive you to the bar, then he'll come back for us."

Curtis hesitated for a moment, then nodded. "Okay."

Frankie turned and walked back inside. A few moments later, Joe emerged from the front of the house.

"Let's go," he said without breaking stride. "I've got to drop you off then get back."

They climbed into the car, Joe driving, and left the house.

Neither said anything as they drove. They drove into the downtown area. They passed the butcher shop which had once been owned by Sam Marino, a small grocery store, a movie store, and finally pulled up to Randall's Tavern. A sign hung down from a black metal pole that stuck out over the corner. It was red brick with a door that was more modern than the rest of the building.

Joe parked and let Curtis climb out.

"Sure you don't need anything else?" said Joe, leaning across the center console. "Protection or anything?"

"No thanks," said Curtis. "Go back and get Frankie and Officer Oberman."

"Yes, sir," said Joe without much enthusiasm.

As the car did a U-turn and disappeared into the distance, Curtis looked up at the bar. He stepped inside and blinked to adjust his eyes to the dim light. The bar wouldn't have looked out of place in a western movie save for the LED lights hanging from the ceiling and the six flat screens above the bar, playing MLB and NFL highlights.

"Curtis Mackley!" shouted the bartender, making the patrons look at him then at Curtis, trying to match his face to the former chief of police. "Welcome back!"

Curtis smiled at Robert Randall, the proprietor of the bar

for as long as Curtis could remember. Robert met Curtis at the end of the bar with a broad smile.

Curtis held out a hand, and Robert shook it.

The bartender had a Santa Claus vibe about him, with the right body type and a thick white beard which had been brown the last time Curtis had seen him.

"Great to see you again, lad," said Robert. "I only wish it was under better circumstances."

"You and me both," said Curtis. "Who told you I was coming in?"

"You know Natasha Nolowinski? The reporter for the Blind River Observer?"

"Yeah," said Curtis, a sinking feeling in his gut. "I've met her."

Robert leaned over the bar. "Natasha came in here and told us all. Great news that the feds are taking an interest in those girls, and even more so that one of our own is taking care of it. I was so relieved to hear it was a local. When she said it, well, I didn't believe her. I was saying to myself, 'little Curtis Mackley? An FBI agent? That can't be right.' But here you are. My god, I can't believe someone from this little town rose all the way up to being in the FBI. Hey, fellas, would you have guessed that Curtis here would be an FBI agent?"

The responses were a few disinterested grunts from the men at the bar before they looked back at the televisions. One man muttered that the girls had probably just run away and Curtis was wasting his time, but neither Robert nor the other bar patrons paid him any attention.

"Anyway, lad," said Robert, turning back to Curtis as he took a seat. "What'll you have?"

"A glass of whatever you've got on tap."

"You got it." Robert got him a glass of beer. He placed it on the bar in front of Curtis.

Curtis took a sip. "You remember you used to slip us beers when we were teenagers? First beer I ever drank came from that fridge right over there."

"Oh, I remember, lad. Kids loved me."

"You still do that?" said Curtis. "You know any of the girls who disappeared?"

"Nah, lad. Police wised up to what I was doing about eight years back. Got slapped with an enormous fine for serving alcohol to minors. Almost put me out of business. I'm not making that mistake again."

"That's a shame," said Curtis.

"I agree. I always figured it was better they get beers here than drugs somewhere else. How is the investigation to find those girls going? I really wish I could be more help."

"I'm not able to speak about that with people outside the investigation."

"Oh, that's fine." Robert seemed to have deflated, and Curtis felt guilty about his lack of information.

"How's Debra?" said Curtis.

That seemed to deflate Robert even more. "Oh, she passed a few years back, lad. Cancer is a rough thing. I've got my son to take care of the bar with me. Otherwise, I'd be at a loss." Robert let out a weak, forced laugh, then sighed. "I've got to check on the other customers. Let me know if you need anything."

Robert retreated to the other side of the bar and started talking with one of the other patrons.

Curtis sipped his beer and looked up at the screens, not

absorbing anything. Somewhere in the background a door opened and closed.

A figure blocked Curtis's view of the screen. It took him a second to focus on the man standing behind the bar.

The man was in his mid-twenties. He had scars criss-crossing his forehead and underneath his tight shirt. He had both hands on the bar in front of him and was staring at Curtis.

"Hi, Bobby," said Curtis, recognizing Robert's son. "What's up?"

"You shouldn't be here," said Bobby. "Come with me."

Curtis sipped at the beer then followed Bobby to the end of the bar. Bobby led Curtis to a corner table out of earshot of the other patrons.

Curtis took a seat opposite Bobby, making sure he had a few different avenues of escape if he needed it.

Curtis said, "What do you want to talk to me about?"

"Marino knows it was you," said Bobby.

Curtis felt his heart skip a beat. "What?"

"Marino knows it was you who ratted him out to the cops."

"How?"

Bobby leaned in. "I was in that prison for a few months," he said. "DUI, robbery, stuff piled up. Everyone in there knows Marino has it out for an FBI agent who fucked him over. Thinking about one day killing you is what keeps Marino going. When he finds out you're back in town, I wouldn't want to be you."

Curtis tried to remain calm. "Why does he think I did it?"

Bobby leaned back. "From what I hear, the moment he found out you were an FBI agent he put it together. Something about you being a paperboy and wearing a wire. I didn't get all the details, but I'm sure Marino knows."

Curtis nodded and sipped at his beer. "Thanks for telling me. I appreciate it."

"Just remember this if I ever need anything," said Bobby with a smirk. He stood and walked back to the bar.

Curtis wondered what he was going to do about Marino. He still had connections in Blind River outside the prison, far more than Curtis had. He had once tortured and killed a man who had threatened his growing empire.

Curtis had destroyed that same empire.

CHAPTER 11

FRANKIE ARRIVED AT THE BAR TWENTY MINUTES LATER AND SAT opposite Curtis.

"We can safely assume Kelly Oberman isn't a suspect," she said.

"Why?" said Curtis, looking at the empty glass in front of him.

"She's got an alibi, and I can't see her doing it. She's a mother, and she's fought tooth and nail for those kids. She's got quite a story. She opened up to me once you left. Might have been a woman thing. She got pregnant in her first year of University and lived with her grandmother while she finished school. When her grandmother died, Kelly was given the house in her will. She raised Matt and Darcy there. They have different fathers, in case you were wondering."

Curtis nodded. "She has an alibi?"

"She was at volleyball practice the night Darcy disappeared. We'll check, but it's probably bulletproof."

"What about the fathers?"

"I sent their info to the FBI to check them out, but Kelly

doesn't suspect them. Neither has any connection with their child."

"Any suspects?" Curtis said as he waved down Robert and held his glass in the air.

Robert pointed at Frankie and gave her a questioning glance. She shook her head.

"No suspects yet," said Frankie, turning back to Curtis. "We need to start looking through the list of suspects Monica, and Trevor put together. The butterfly hairclip is the only physical evidence. We might need to wait for another kidnapping."

Robert brought Curtis's beer and asked Frankie again if she wanted anything.

"A glass of water would be great," she said.

"Coming right up."

Robert returned with Frankie's water. Curtis waited for him to be out of earshot before continuing the conversation.

"The kidnapper must know that the FBI is here," he said.

"If this guy could stop, he'd have stopped after Ashley Hagerty," said Frankie. "How long would it have taken before people realized she hadn't run away from home? Weeks? Months? That's enough time to completely uproot a life and start somewhere else. Someone else is going to get kidnapped. This guy isn't done yet. That's why we need to speak at the school."

Curtis nodded. "There's no other way?"

"Not that I can think of."

"If the girls are still alive," said Curtis, "we need to be doing everything in our power to find them."

"We'll find them," said Frankie, "one way or another."

Curtis nodded, although he didn't share Frankie's optimism. There were too many cases where they hadn't found the victims, where the perpetrator was never caught, and where the families never got closure.

"So, tell me about this sibling of yours who disappeared," said Frankie.

Curtis looked away. With Bobby's declaration about Marino, he had forgotten what happened at the Obermans' house.

"His name was Josh," said Curtis. "He disappeared twenty-five years ago, without a trace. He went to bed one night, and the next morning he wasn't there. The window wasn't open, there was nothing to indicate force had been used. He left of his own free will and never came back. I was ten at the time. Josh was twenty. I always assumed it was Marino's fault, that Josh had been working for him without us knowing, and something had gone south."

Frankie nodded. "Is that why you--?"

"Why I joined the FBI or why I wore the wire to catch Marino?"

Frankie shrugged. "Both, I guess."

Curtis shrugged. "Yeah."

"The police never found anything to suggest what happened to Josh?"

"No."

"So he could have run away? He could still be alive?"

Curtis nodded. "I haven't heard anything from him. Twenty-five years, Frankie. We weren't close, but we were brothers. It's easier to assume he's dead."

Frankie looked at him for a moment, then checked her watch. "We need to get to dinner. Thank you for telling me this."

"Are you going to tell Johnson? He doesn't know that part of it."

Frankie stood and dropped a few bills on the table. "I haven't decided yet."

"Let me know when you do."

"I will."

Curtis waved to Robert as they exited the bar and walked out to their new car. Frankie explained she had dropped off Matt and Joe at the station and taken the new car Chief Tucker had supplied to them so they wouldn't have to use his car anymore.

As they left the downtown area, Curtis muttered, "I should never have come back."

"You can leave anytime," said Frankie. "I'm sure Johnson would understand."

Curtis looked out the window at the houses passing by. They were headed to his father's for dinner, the first such dinner in almost two decades.

"No, let's finish this," he said. "The house on the right here."

CHAPTER 12

THE HOUSE WAS MODEST WITH A SMALL YARD. MONICA'S CAR was already in the driveway.

Curtis knocked on the door of his childhood home. It occurred to him as they stood on the porch that his primary reason for coming to this dinner, to find out if his father knew about his involvement in Marino's arrest, had become irrelevant since his conversation with Bobby Randall.

He reached down and slipped his wedding ring off his finger. It wasn't a topic he wanted to cover tonight. There were too many questions. He wondered momentarily if Monica had already noticed the ring.

Monica opened the door, and they stepped inside.

"Dad's in the living room," said Monica. "He wants to see you."

Trevor was sitting in the kitchen reading a newspaper. He nodded to Curtis when he saw him.

Curtis returned the nod and walked into the living room. Gordon Mackley was sitting on the couch, watching a baseball game. He looked well for a man nearing seventy-five. He had had his children late in life after he had already established himself as a force to be reckoned with in the Blind River Police Department. Only Josh had been born before he became chief.

"Hey, Dad," said Curtis.

There was no reply.

"Dad?"

"He doesn't respond too well anymore," said Monica, stepping up beside him. She had a somber expression. "Here, I'll get him to talk to you."

Monica walked in front of the television, blocking their father's view of the game. "Dad? Curtis is here to see you."

"Curtis?" said Gordon.

"Your son."

"Josh?"

"No, Curtis."

Curtis stepped beside her. "Hey, Dad."

"Yes, of course, I remember Curtis," said Gordon. "How are you doing?"

Curtis stepped forward and hugged his father. The returned hug was hesitant and uncertain, as though he wasn't sure Curtis was real.

"You look good, Dad," said Curtis.

"Thanks. You look pretty good yourself," said Gordon. "How's your brother?"

Curtis looked at Monica, who shook her head. He turned back and said, "He's doing fine."

"Good, very good. Good to see you."

Curtis nodded and left him to watch the game.

He walked with Monica to the kitchen, where Frankie and Trevor were having a conversation about the kidnappings. Trevor was explaining their list of suspects, and about how they had too many. It was currently 200 people long, and none of the suspects stood out.

"So, what's up with him?" said Curtis as he took his seat, nodding to his father.

"Age-induced Dementia and Alzheimer's," said Monica, taking her seat. "Nothing particularly unusual, according to the doctors. He's just old."

"Are they still taking care of him?"

Monica sighed. "I'm paying for a nurse to visit a few times a day most of the week. I'm here on the weekends. He's still able to take care of himself. His habits are fine. It's the details he can't remember. The gaps in his memory are random and inconsistent. Some days he remembers Josh, sometimes he doesn't."

Curtis nodded, unsure what to say.

"Don't say anything, Curtis," said Monica. "You've done enough damage already just by not being here."

Monica stood and walked to the stove, where dinner, steak, and potatoes, was cooking.

Curtis sighed. "Do you know where we're staying tonight?"

"For tonight," said Trevor, breaking into the conversation, "you're staying at Monica's. We'll try to get something set up for tomorrow night, but the motels are booked, and my house is too small."

"No problem," said Curtis.

Dinner was served.

Monica led Gordon into the kitchen to his seat. They spoke about the case, throwing ideas back and forth only to have Monica and Trevor shoot them down, saying they'd already thought of that.

Almost every criminal within a fifty-mile radius had no motive and the few who might had alibis. They kept coming back to the simple fact that the culprit probably had no motive. Instead, he was doing it out of some sick urge.

Frankie went to use the bathroom and stopped by the kitchen on the way back. "Anyone want a drink?"

"I'll have a beer," said Curtis. Monica held up two fingers to indicate she wanted one as well.

"Trevor?" said Frankie.

He shook his head. "Just water. I quit drinking."

Frankie nodded. "Good for you."

"Where's Barb?" said Gordon as Frankie sat down and handed out the drinks. After almost half an hour of silence and playing with the food on his plate, Gordon Mackley was looking for the woman who had died three decades prior. "Barb?"

Monica laid a hand on his arm. "She's gone, Dad. Remember?"

"Yes, of course," said Gordon, looking around. "I thought she was here. Never mind." He continued to look around, as though unsure if it was all a big joke. "How's Nate?" he said after a moment.

"He's fine," said Monica.

"Why isn't he here?"

"We broke up, Dad."

"Who's Nate?" said Curtis.

"Her ex-husband," said Trevor.

Curtis frowned. "You were married?"

Monica pinched the bridge of her nose and let out an exasperated breath. "Nate Williams. You remember him?"

"Yeah, he was a football player. I remember him."

Trevor glared at Curtis.

"We got married after two months of dating," said Monica. "He works at the prison, and I happened to be there a lot. It was a mistake. We got divorced after six months. That's all there is to it."

"If you say so," said Trevor, making eye contact with Curtis.

Monica turned to her brother. "Curtis, is there anyone in your life?"

Curtis picked up some steak with his fork. He put it in his mouth, chewed, and swallowed. "Yeah, we've been together for a while. Her name is Melanie."

"Is it serious?"

Curtis put his right hand into his pocket, playing with the wedding ring there. The detectives must have noticed it earlier in the day. He could feel Frankie watching him. "I don't know," he finally answered. "Maybe."

Frankie exhaled and looked at him, but said nothing.

"I liked Nate!" said Gordon loudly, as though making sure he would be heard.

CHAPTER 13

FRANKIE LASSITER HAD MISSED HER MORNING WORKOUT DUE TO their flight and was feeling antsy. When dinner finished, she stood and offered to clear the plates off the table as an excuse to move a bit. She'd never understood why people enjoyed sitting.

She did a few dishes until Monica came up behind her and kicked her back to the table.

On her way back through the house, she walked through the hallway adjacent to the bathroom. Pictures hung on both sides of the hall dating back decades.

Frankie found herself moving backward through time as she walked through the hall. The most recent picture depicted Curtis graduating from the police academy with Gordon and Monica in tow.

As she moved down the wall, she went through high school, where they'd played multiple sports. Monica played for Kelly Oberman's soccer team one year.

About halfway through the hall, another person joined

the family, seemingly out of nowhere. The picture depicted a summer camping trip, with the Mackleys sitting around a fire pit. Curtis was about ten, and Monica was a few years younger. Gordon, clear-eyed and smiling, stood nearby.

Josh Mackley looked to be around twenty. He had long brown hair and tattoos running down his arms. He looked happy and unbothered, yet this was the last picture of him before he disappeared into thin air.

She continued moving down the wall, into the past, where Josh was present in every photo and at every major life event which the Mackleys had experienced. When Curtis was around five, a woman--Frankie assumed this must be Barbara--joined the group, then it ended when Monica was being held in her mother's arms.

Frankie wondered what had happened to Barbara. Curtis had never mentioned his mother; then again, he hadn't mentioned his family at all until they had arrived in Blind River.

"Frankie?"

She turned. Trevor was standing at the end of the hallway.

"We're going to get going," said Trevor. "I just wanted to let you know in case you needed directions. Curtis knows where he's going." He looked at the wall, then walked up to her. "It's strange, isn't it? I always found it a little odd they kept all these pictures on the wall like they're clinging to the past."

"What do you think happened to Josh?" said Frankie. "You've lived here your entire life. You must have known him."

Trevor looked up at the wall. "Not personally. The first I

heard of him was when he disappeared. Chief's son disappeared, and the town was helpless to do anything about it. It was the first time people understood how powerful Marino had become. As to what happened, my guess is no better than anyone else's. Monica doesn't talk about it, and I've never gone through the old files."

"Curtis seems concerned about Marino. Is there any credence to that?"

Trevor shrugged. "Again, your guess is as good as mine." Someone honked outside in the driveway. "I've got to go."

Trevor walked to the front door with Frankie following. Gordon was back in his chair in the living room, a tray of drinks and snacks beside him. "Is he alright alone?" said Frankie.

Trevor said, "He'll be fine. A nurse will be here in an hour or so. He'll be fine until then."

Frankie followed Trevor out the door but felt uneasy about leaving the former chief alone. Frankie looked back at the house one more time as she climbed into the driver's seat of their car. Curtis was already sitting in the passenger seat.

They pulled out of the driveway behind Monica and Trevor's car.

"Did you learn anything?" said Frankie.

"What?" Curtis looked back at her.

"About Marino. Did your dad know about it?"

"No, he doesn't know anything," said Curtis. "I don't think Condra ever told him. We don't have to worry about him. Not in that way, anyway."

They pulled into the driveway of a two-story house behind Monica's car.

Monica walked to the front door and unlocked it.

Frankie and Curtis grabbed their luggage from the trunk of Monica's car and walked inside.

The inside of the house was decorated sparsely, as though Monica had never bothered to unpack. The only noticeable difference from a regular house was the bullet hole above the basement door.

"What happened there?" said Curtis, indicating the hole.

"Nothing important," said Monica dismissively. "There's an extra bedroom upstairs. Then there's the couch. It's not a pull-out, sorry."

"I'll take the couch," said Curtis. "Don't worry about it."

Frankie knew Curtis was trying to be a gentleman, and she hated that, but she wasn't about to turn down a bed. She turned to Monica. "Is there anywhere I can get a work out in the morning?"

Monica thought for a moment. "There's a gym downtown. I can give you directions."

"Thanks," said Frankie.

Curtis fell onto the couch. "We should meet at nine tomorrow morning and bring everyone up to speed. We'll probably spend most of tomorrow interviewing the families and speaking at the school."

Frankie nodded. "I'm going to get some sleep. I want to work out in the morning."

Frankie said her good nights and walked upstairs.

She listened to the sounds of the house and the town, feeling an unclear dread. She'd lived in cities her entire life, and the silence of this town unnerved her. She could hear the wind blowing through the backyards and a dog barking in the distance. She was waiting for a noise that would never come.

How anyone could live in a town this small, she would never understand.

CHAPTER 14

CURTIS BLINKED AND STRETCHED HIS BACK. IT WAS STILL DARK outside, the only lights coming from the houses across the street. He grabbed his phone from the coffee table and checked the time. 5:00 AM.

"Shit," he muttered. He tried to reposition himself on the couch, wishing he had taken the bed, knowing Frankie wouldn't have argued with him.

After half an hour of staring at the ceiling trying to fall asleep, he chalked it up to a lost cause and sat up. The silence of the town soothed him, reminded him how loud and disruptive the city had seemed to him when he had first moved to New York to join the police force there. He'd worked as a New York cop for seven years before joining the FBI.

When he was sure he heard nothing in the house except his own breathing, he made a phone call to a number he had looked up on the flight. He set up a meeting at 7:30 AM.

He grabbed the car keys of their borrowed car and left a

note for Frankie. She would be angry, but she wouldn't call Johnson over this.

He needed to do this. He hadn't wanted to come to Blind River, but now that he was here he may as well make the most of it.

He pulled out of the driveway, looking back at the house once more as the car clunked onto the road, then turned east. He drove through Blind River, and in that morning tranquility, he saw the town in which he had grown up. The air felt the same as he remembered, the sun rose in the same spot, and the emptiness of the downtown area was peaceful in a way that big city folk would never understand. He drove out of the downtown area and back toward the airfield.

He turned toward the Blind River Maximum Security Penitentiary.

His FBI identification got him through security with no issues.

"Go inside, sir," said the last guard, buzzing him in. "Take a seat at one of the tables and the prisoner will be with you shortly."

"Thanks," said Curtis. "I believe the warden wanted to speak with me."

"He'll be here in about half an hour. He told us to let you speak to the prisoner first."

Curtis nodded and stepped inside. He took a seat on the close side of the table.

A few minutes later, the door on the other side opened, and a guard led Sam Marino into the interview room.

Marino's eyes widened when he saw Curtis. The guard was also familiar to Curtis, a young man named Harry Ochre he had attended high school with. He nodded to Harry in acknowledgment.

"So, Curtis Mackley," said Marino, taking his seat as Harry attached his cuffs to the table. "I didn't expect to ever see you again. What brings you here?"

Curtis looked at Marino for a few moments while Harry retreated to the door. He would watch through the window in case there were any issues, but their conversation, per the agreement Curtis had made with the warden, would be private.

Marino had let himself go while in prison, and the years hadn't been kind to him. While once he had been fit and healthy, able to fight his own battles, and with a full head of luscious black hair, he was now fat, his jowls jutting out from his orange prison shirt, and his scalp showing through where he had combed his grey hair over.

"I'm with the FBI," said Curtis, speaking in a professional manner. "FBI Special Agent Curtis Mackley. I'm here investigating some disappearances."

"Huh," said Marino, squinting at the identification Curtis held up. "Isn't that interesting? Who disappeared?"

Curtis stared at Marino. He had never been one to hide his emotions, but he seemed calm now. Curtis had prepared himself for death threats or worse, but Marino didn't even seem annoyed.

Marino tilted his head to one side.

"Four high school girls from Blind River," said Curtis. "All taken in the middle of the night, no trace of them except a butterfly hairclip. Have you heard anything about that?"

"I think I've heard something about that." Marino leaned

forward. "Why come to me, Curtis? I've been locked up for almost twenty years."

"We both know you still have connections and resources. The FBI has been keeping tabs on your movements. We know you're still operating."

Marino hesitated for a moment, then broke into a deep laugh. "You almost had me for a moment there, Curtis."

"Are you sure? There's a large quantity of cocaine moving around the northeast that bears your signature."

"No, there isn't," said Marino. "I would know about it."

Curtis shrugged. "Our information seems to indicate otherwise. Come on, Sam, you always referred to yourself as a businessman. Think of this as one businessman to another. What reason do you have not to trust me?"

"You're a fucking FBI agent," said Marino. "Bunch of selfish pricks is what you are. I know exactly what this is. You're trying to trick me to get information about those girls. You really think I'm that stupid?"

"Only if you don't believe me."

Marino paused for a moment. "You were always a prick, Curtis. Figures you'd end up working for the kingdom of pricks. Tell me about the girls."

Curtis did, telling him everything except their names, including where they'd disappeared.

When he finished, Marino grinned broadly and started laughing. "I thought you were supposed to be smart. Looks like the FBI made a mistake in picking you."

Curtis leaned in. "What are you talking about?"

Marino leaned back with that same smug smile Curtis had always associated with him. "Bring me the information on the cocaine. Maybe I'll tell you who's kidnapping and murdering those girls. I'd like to go back to my cell now."

Marino raised a hand to signal Harry, who came back in, unlocked him from the table, and led him out of the room.

He didn't look back at Curtis, who was left alone in the interview room.

Curtis left with more questions than he'd come with. He let out a grunt before walking out of the interview room.

A guard was there, waiting to take him to the warden's office. He introduced himself as Nate Williams, and Curtis shook his hand. This was the man Monica had been married to. He seemed normal if a bit boring. Nate made no mention of this connection, and neither did Curtis.

Nate took him to a bank of elevators, which he activated using a special key card and a code. They rode the elevator up three floors and exited into a red-carpeted hallway lined by portraits of past wardens.

Nate knocked on the door at the end of the hall while Curtis waited. A deep voice from inside told them to enter.

The door opened, and Curtis stepped into an immaculate office with one wall of windows looking out over the entire prison. The door closed behind him.

He introduced himself and took his seat across from the warden.

Warden Thompson defied the typical look of prison wardens. He was tall, muscular, and handsome.

"Sorry I wasn't here to meet you," said Warden Thompson. "I'm sure you understand I wasn't expecting a call from the FBI this morning. I assume you're investigating the disappearances of those girls."

"Yes," said Curtis. "Do you live in Blind River?"

"I have a house there. I have a place in Albany as well, where I stay on my days off. It's a tragedy what happened to those girls, but I have to ask what the connection is to Marino. He's been in prison for almost twenty years. He isn't eligible for parole for another ten."

"I don't know," said Curtis. "He must still have connections. And there are still questions he never answered which I wanted to ask."

"I haven't heard anything," said Thompson, "but I don't spend a lot of time with the prisoners. You'd be better off asking the guards who work with the general population."

Curtis looked over the prison yard. The sun was rising above the walls of the prison. Frankie would be waking up and finding his note.

"What do you think about Marino?" he said.

"He's smart," said Thompson. "He knows who he can control and who he can't. He can get most of what he wants, but he's still in prison, and he knows that. There are guys here who don't give two shits about hierarchy or power. They'll have their way with him if he steps on the wrong toes."

"Nothing suspicious, though? No indications at an escape attempt?"

"No." Thompson frowned. "Do you think he's going to try?"

"Just a hunch."

Thompson nodded. "We'll check out his cell. An FBI agent's hunch is worth something."

"Thank you for your time." Curtis stood, checking his watch. "I need to get back. If I need to, I'll be back to interview some of the guards. Let the guards who are closest to Marino know."

Thompson stood and shook his hand again. "I won't be able to take them away from their duties for too long. We're understaffed as it is."

"Can't you hire more guards?"

"It doesn't work like that," said Thompson. "We can train them, but it's impossible to tell who'll be able to handle the job. Most of the guards who quit do so in the first week, then we need to start the entire process over."

"I won't take long if I speak to them."

"Thank you."

Curtis walked out of the office, back down the hall to the elevator with Nate and out to his car.

It was only once he was back on the highway, looking at the prison in his rearview mirror, that he let out the breath he hadn't realized he'd been holding.

CHAPTER 15

Frankie stretched her legs, then her arms. She jogged on the spot for a few seconds and made sure her iPhone was hooked up to her headphones. The sun was just starting to rise over the trees, the perfect time to go for a run. Some FBI agents wore their guns while they worked out, they felt naked without it, but Frankie didn't like the way it bounced against her hip when she ran. Instead, she wore a knife on her thigh.

She walked down the stairs and into the kitchen.

She tried to tiptoe so as not to wake Curtis, but the couch where he had slept was empty. She picked up the note on top of the folded sheets, scanned it, then crumpled it up.

She would talk to him later.

She left the house and took off at a jog, Kanye West playing in her ears.

She got to the gym in less than half an hour, the sun shining on her back as she arrived. She bought a day pass from the front desk, drank a Gatorade, and walked inside. There was a stack of free newspapers sitting on a rack. The Blind River Observer sat on the top shelf of the rack. Frankie felt her stomach contorting into a knot as she read the headline.

"FBI agents called in to help find runaway girls," read the headline. The author was Natasha Nolowinski.

Frankie grabbed a paper and unfolded it, revealing a picture of Curtis and her emerging from the Hagertys home with Officer Hagerty and Officer Oberman. As she read the article, Frankie could feel her blood boiling. It read:

"Chief Tucker and the Blind River Police Department have never been known for their skill in solving cases, but their incompetence reached a new level on Wednesday, as they called in the Federal Bureau of Investigation to solve a solved case. The case of the missing girls has been universally agreed to be the coincidental running away of teenage girls from overprotective and controlling parents. There are no crimes involved, and it is a waste of taxpayer dollars for the police, let alone the FBI, to try to find them. Ashley Hagerty, Miranda O'Connell, Darcy Oberman, and Harriet Matheson 'disappeared' over the last several weeks. The disappearances were all drastically different, and the girls didn't associate with one another outside of classes.

"Making matters worse is the potential ulterior motive of FBI Agent Curtis Mackley, the son of former chief Gordon Mackley and sister of police detective Monica Mackley, the lead detective on the disappearances. Curtis Mackley is reputed to be obsessed with connecting the case with Sam Marino, a former crime boss serving a fifty-year sentence in Blind River Penitentiary.

"The best course of action for the police and the FBI is to stop investigating this case, stop listening to the hysterical parents of missing girls, and pretend it never happened. If they don't, when the girls reappear, this will look bad on everyone involved, including (Continued on page 4)"

Frankie scrunched up the newspaper in her hands. She remembered Natasha from the previous day and locked the image in her memory. She tossed the newspaper into the garbage can and did her workout, trying to channel her anger.

When she was finished, she wiped off her brow, grabbed another copy of the newspaper to show to Curtis and the detectives, and walked the few miles back to the house, the sun shining in her eyes.

When she arrived, the car she and Curtis had been given was in the driveway.

Inside, Curtis was sitting at the counter eating toast.

"Trevor and Monica will meet us at the station," he said.

Frankie glared at him. "I'm having a shower, and then you're going to do two things. One, you are going to tell me everything that happened with Marino."

He nodded. "And second?"

"Explain this." She threw the Blind River Observer onto the counter in front of him. She walked past him, only glancing back to see Curtis frown as he began to read.

When she returned from the shower wearing a fresh suit and toweling off her short hair, Curtis was pacing back and forth across the living room, leaving footprints in the carpet, cursing Natasha Nolowinski.

"Is any of it true?" said Frankie.

"No," said Curtis. "Well, she doesn't know the parts that are true. It's educated guesses."

"What parts are true?"

Curtis hesitated, stopping his pacing and standing in place.

"One phone call to Johnson," said Frankie.

Curtis nodded. He told her about Bobby Randall's information and his meeting with Marino.

"Marino's probably bluffing me just like I bluffed him," said Curtis when he finished, "but we can't take that risk. He ruled this town for almost a decade. He's bound to still have connections. He knows something."

Frankie nodded. "I'll call Johnson and get some verifiable information about the drug trade in the northeast. You can trade it with Marino for information. Until then, we need to focus on the ongoing investigation, and assume for the time being that Marino knows nothing."

"I need to speak with Bobby Randall again," said Curtis. "I should do that alone."

"Keep me informed on this," said Frankie. "I mean, it, Curtis."

Curtis nodded.

CHAPTER 16

THEY ARRIVED AT THE STATION AT EIGHT-THIRTY. NATASHA WAS standing outside the door, her camera and notepad ready.

"What do you have to say about the allegations made in the Blind River Observer?" said Natasha as she walked up to them.

"You mean the article you wrote?" said Frankie without breaking stride. "We'll be taking legal action for defamation and a breach of journalistic ethics."

"What would that be?" said Natasha.

Frankie stopped at the door to the station. Curtis stood behind her.

"All the allegations made in the paper are wrong," said Frankie. "Every piece of evidence we have indicates that the girls were kidnapped, and your newspaper is intentionally lying to sell copies."

They stepped inside and slammed the door, shutting out Natasha's shouted questions.

"She has no shame," said Curtis, "does she?"

"Doesn't seem like it," said Frankie. "They're waiting for us."

They walked through the station to the war room.

Trevor and Monica looked up from their conversation when the two of them entered. Chief Tucker followed and took up his seat at the back of the room. It almost seemed like Tucker was intentionally taking a background role to let Monica and Trevor run the show.

"So," said Trevor, "what are your initial impressions?"

Curtis looked at the whiteboard. "Despite what the newspaper said this morning, we believe that the kidnappings are connected. The M.O. is too similar, and the chance of all four girls disappearing in such a short time is essentially zero."

Trevor nodded. "Ignore Nolowinski. We all do. She thinks she deserves to be a big city reporter and doesn't understand it takes a certain amount of honesty and integrity to get there. She has her followers, but no one takes them seriously."

Curtis continued. "We believe the person committing these crimes is a local. He's doing it not because he wants to, but because he's addicted to the feeling of it. Eventually, he'll try again. That's the best chance we have to catch him. He's probably done it before, but not here. The FBI will be looking through similar unsolved cases in New York and surrounding states. Frankie and I will be finishing our interviews with the families today. Have you made arrangements for us to speak at the school?"

Trevor nodded. "This afternoon. The friends of the victims will be available to speak with you one on one afterward."

"Thanks," said Curtis. "We'll need Officer Hagerty and Officer Oberman to come with us again. Try narrowing down the list of suspects. The FBI will be sending lists of similar unsolved crimes within five hundred miles. We need the list as short as possible. Any questions?"

Monica said, "What's happening with Marino? Nolowinski must be basing that line in the paper off something, right?"

Curtis shrugged. "I spoke to him at the prison this morning. He claims to know who the killer is, but I think he's bluffing. The FBI is setting up some information to trade with him. Frankie and I are going to head out. Let us know if we're needed for any reason."

Monica nodded. She leaned back and crossed her arms.

They left Monica and Trevor at the station, ignored Natasha's onslaught of questions as they walked to their car, and drove away. Curtis leaned back and watched Natasha as they pulled away, thankful she didn't follow. They met up with Joe and Matt and proceeded to the next house.

CHAPTER 17

They arrived at the O'Connell house around ten. It was a one-story house with a perfect lawn and plants that were cut in a way that resembled modern art.

The door was answered by a man who looked like he had dressed up for the occasion. He wore a white dress shirt, his pants perfectly hemmed, his hair cut to perfection. He wore a somber expression as they made their introductions. He was Gareth O'Connell, Miranda's father.

The inside of the house was equally perfect. Frankie felt guilty for the small amount of mud that came off her shoes as she stepped on the welcome mat. She saw Gareth glance at it, but he made no comment. They removed their shoes and walked inside.

In the living room, a tray filled with snacks and coffee was waiting for them. There were pictures along the wall of their family. A mother, a father, a daughter. It looked like a normal family, but not quite, as though it was a family of mannequins instead of humans.

A woman, who introduced herself as Reba O'Connell,

shook their hands as they entered. She wore a blue pantsuit and stood with the same poise and confidence her husband exuded. They sat beside one another on the couch.

Frankie couldn't help but think they looked like clones of one another. They sat with their knees together and their hands folded in their laps.

The two officers stood in the doorway, not wanting to remove their shoes in case they had to leave urgently, but also not wanting to plod any dirt onto the flawless, almost mirror-like floors.

"Thank you for meeting with us," said Curtis as they took their seats. "I'm sure this is difficult for you."

"We're just thankful that the FBI is doing everything they can to help," said Reba. There was a politician's cadence to her words. "Anything we can do to help find Miranda, we are more than willing to do."

"What can you tell us about the last day you saw her?" said Curtis. "Anything can be helpful. Details are where these cases always come together."

"Let's see," said Reba, speaking like she was the applicant in a job interview instead of a mother speaking about her missing daughter. "I dropped her off for piano lessons on the night she disappeared. We'd heard about the kidnappings, but hadn't thought much of it. The other two girls were so different from Miranda. We couldn't fathom that anyone would want to attack her. She's wanted to quit piano for about a year now, but we aren't a family of quitters. If she wants to get into an Ivy school, then she's going to need some extra-curricular activities." Reba trailed off and looked blankly at the empty air above the coffee table. For the first time, she looked like a terrified mother.

Her husband took over. "She normally gets a ride home from her piano teacher's house," said Gareth. "but that night she decided to walk. Her teacher said she was adamant about it. When she didn't come home, we thought she was just throwing a fit. She was still trying to quit the lessons and destroy her future. When she wasn't home by ten, we got worried. That's her curfew on nights when she has lessons. It's nine otherwise, no exceptions. We're not the kind of parents who let their kids run around doing whatever they want. They're too young and too immature. They make bad decisions and could destroy their lives. She'll thank us in the future."

Curtis cleared his throat. "You were talking about when she wasn't home by curfew."

"Right," said Gareth, looking at the ground. "When she didn't come home, we got worried. We called the police, and they came immediately." He let out a cry, his façade of a calm, collected, unbothered man coming undone. "I'm sorry. I just want to know what happened. Do either of you have children?"

Curtis and Frankie shook their heads.

"No," said Curtis. "That's why we brought the two officers here. They're both family members of the missing girls."

Gareth's eyes looked at the two men in the hallway.

Reba seemed comatose, staring straight ahead.

"Don't worry about the floors," said Gareth, defeated. "Come in. I want to talk to someone who understands."

Joe and Matt walked into the living room, trailing dirt along the clean floors. They sat in the remaining chairs.

"Have you been able to sleep?" said Gareth.

Both officers shook their heads.

Gareth wiped his tears with his sleeve. "I just want to be awake in case she calls or if she needs my help. I can't keep going like this."

Matt stood and walked over to him. He pulled the man into an embrace. Gareth hugged him back, and the embrace lasted for a few moments. Gareth was now weeping openly.

When Matt released him, Gareth made an obvious excuse about needing to get back to work. Reba O'Connell said nothing. Gareth put a hand on his wife's shoulder. She nodded, her lips pressed tight together.

Curtis and Frankie thanked them.

Gareth and Reba managed to regain some of their composure as they stood in the doorway, thanking them and saying goodbye. They promised they would do everything they possibly could to help the police and the FBI find the missing girls. They looked professional, more like a team of lawyers than parents of a missing child, but the vacant stares showed their pain.

They all climbed back into the car.

Frankie thanked the two officers, both of whom muttered responses while they stared out the back windows.

They turned onto the road and headed toward the last house.

CHAPTER 18

"You didn't mention the hairclip?" said Joe from the back seat of the car.

"Things like can break a family," said Frankie. "We want them to talk. Sometimes details make it too real. If the hairclip becomes a key part of the investigation, we'll go back and ask them."

"It's the only physical evidence?" said Joe.

"That we have right now."

"Then why not ask them about it?"

"We need them to remember this interview as a positive event that contributed to finding their daughter."

Oberman looked out the window as they turned toward the last house. "That's why you brought us?"

"Yes," said Frankie.

"We're here," said Curtis, pointing to a house on the right. The Matheson's house was the polar opposite of the O'Connell's.

It was a blue house with peeling paint and overgrown grass. A rusting tricycle sat in the middle of the lawn, matching the paint job of the pickup truck in the driveway.

They knocked twice. A twenty-something woman answered the door. She had dark eyeliner and greasy hair. A cigarette hung from between her nicotine-stained fingers. She looked them up and down, took a drag on the cigarette, let the smoke float into the air between them, and said, "You the federal people looking for Harriet?"

"Yes," said Curtis. "And you are?"

"I'm Kendra, Harriet's sister."

Curtis nodded and introduced the others one at a time. Kendra's dark eyes flitted between them as they were introduced. Frankie got a sense of an unrealized intelligence lurking just beneath the surface.

"Can we come in?" said Curtis.

"Why not?" Kendra shrugged and turned. They followed her into the house, trailing dirt along the dust-covered floors.

"Dad!" Kendra shouted upstairs. "The law's here about Harriet."

"One minute!" came the shout from the second floor. "I'm on the shitter!"

Kendra nodded toward the kitchen. "Sit in there. Any of you want a beer?"

"It's eleven in the morning," said Curtis.

"Is that a no?"

"No, thanks."

Kendra's index finger pointed at each of them in turn, and when they had all declined the offer, she walked to the fridge.

The four of them took their seats around the table and waited.

Kendra closed the fridge. She had two beers in each hand.

She placed all four on the table. She opened one and took a sip before placing it back down. She leaned forward on her elbows, a fresh cigarette hanging between her fingers.

"So," she said, "are you going to find Harriet?"

Curtis leaned in. "We're doing everything in our power to find your sister. Agent Lassiter and I are highly skilled and have the training to deal with situations like this. We'll find everything there is to find."

"You mean you'll find her body?" Kendra raised an eyebrow.

Curtis paused for a moment, then said, "If it isn't possible to bring her home alive, then yes."

"Made any progress?"

"If you tell us everything about your sister, and any suspicions you might have, we can find her."

"How is Sam Marino involved?" said Kendra.

Curtis flinched. "Where'd you get that from?"

"The paper this morning. It's cool that you know the town, even if your father is fucking useless."

Joe reached out a hand and put it on Curtis's shoulder. Curtis glanced at it and unclenched his fists.

"You know," said Kendra, "Natasha's a good friend of mine. I trust what she says."

"How can you say that?" said Curtis. "This is your sister we're talking about."

"Harriet thought she was so smart," said Kendra. "Never thanked us for anything. You should quit while you're ahead, just like your sister and that alcoholic partner of hers should have."

Frankie said, "Trevor quit drinking."

Kendra sipped her beer. "No one stays sober forever."

Frankie breathed through her nose.

Curtis glanced at her.

A thin man who looked like an accountant appeared at the bottom of the stairs and lumbered into the kitchen. There were heavy bags under his eyes.

"How you doing?" he said as he stumbled into the room and grabbed the back of Kendra's chair. "I'm Oscar Matheson. Nice to meet you all."

Once they'd made their introductions, Oscar fell into a chair and grabbed one of the beers Kendra had placed on the table between them.

He popped it open and took a long sip.

"So," said Oscar as he put the beer back down and suppressed a burp, "what are you doing to find my daughter?"

Curtis said, "We're doing everything we can. There's a team at FBI headquarters in Manhattan working around the clock to find them."

Oscar nodded slowly. "How can I help?"

"What can you tell us about the day Harriet disappeared?"

"She was out with her friends. Kendra called the cops, not me. I thought Harriet was just doing her thing."

"What is her thing?" said Frankie.

"Oh," said Oscar, "I thought you'd have been told."

"What?"

Oscar shrugged. "Harriet runs away every few months or so on some half-planned life-changing journey. She always comes back. We have an understanding that I don't ask her about it. In return, she doesn't expect me to support her if she fails out of school."

Curtis turned to Kendra. "What made you realize she was missing?"

Kendra took a drag of her cigarette. "She does run off, but she always answers her phone, and even if she doesn't, she calls back within twenty-four hours. She knows I worry about her. This time, she didn't."

Curtis nodded. "Do you mind if I ask where her mother is?"

"Texas, last I heard," said Oscar with a chuckle from the back of his throat. He took another long swig of beer. "She left the kids with me and went off to marry some rich rancher down there. If that isn't the most Texan thing, I don't know what is. I haven't spoken to her in about ten years."

"She doesn't pay child support?" said Curtis.

Oscar laughed. "You're joking, right? You know how hard it is for a single father to get child support? The lawyers say I won't get any sympathy from a jury."

"We don't need her," said Kendra. "We're fine."

Oscar nodded and looked down at his beer. "We're fine."

He finished the beer and opened another, clasping it with two hands. "When you find her, tell Harriet to come home."

"I promise," said Curtis.

"Thank you."

Kendra stood, indicating the interview was over.

Curtis, Frankie, and the two officers followed her lead.

Kendra walked with them to the door. Curtis and the officers walked out to the car, but Frankie looked back just as they were about to leave.

Kendra was leaning against the doorway, as though she had more to say.

Frankie turned back around. "Is there something else?"

CHAPTER 19

FOR THE FIRST TIME, FRANKIE NOTICED THE BAGS UNDER Kendra's eyes.

"You need to find Harriet alive," said Kendra. "I've never seen my dad like this. He never used to drink at all. Since Harriet disappeared, he's lost any will to live. I'm worried he'll drink himself to death. Find her, please."

Frankie put a hand on her shoulder. "We'll find her."

Kendra nodded, then looked away.

"Is there something else?" said Frankie.

Kendra looked up at the sky. "I don't want people to know it was me."

"I won't tell anyone it was you."

"What if there's court or something?"

"If you know something, tell me. Harriet's life may depend on it."

"It might be nothing."

"Kendra."

Kendra met Frankie's gaze. "Talk to Natasha. Not about

the article. I don't know. It might be nothing, but I feel like she knows something."

Frankie nodded. "I'll talk to her. Your name won't come up."

"Find Harriet, please," said Kendra. "Whatever you need, just tell me."

She gave Frankie a quick hug and skittered inside. Frankie waited on the porch for a moment before walking to the car. Halfway there, her phone rang.

She raised one finger to Curtis, who nodded, then answered the call.

"This is Lassiter."

"Frankie, it's Director Johnson. I wanted to check in. How's the investigation going?"

"We just finished interviewing all the families."

"How's Curtis?"

Frankie paused. "In what way, sir?"

"I saw you'd requested we scrounge up some verifiable evidence to trade with Sam Marino. I don't know if Curtis has told you about his history with Marino—"

"He told me," said Frankie, "and if I'm being perfectly candid, Director, I have to ask why you put us on this case."

"You're professionals," said Johnson, "and Curtis knows Blind River better than anyone. However, I see your point. If you think Curtis should be pulled out at any time, we'll send someone else. Understood?"

Frankie looked at Curtis. "He seems fine. I'll let you know if that changes."

"Make sure you do. We'll be sending over the evidence for Marino soon."

Johnson ended the call without saying goodbye, leaving Frankie wondering whether she had just lied to the Director of the FBI.

CHAPTER 20

MONICA AND TREVOR WERE WAITING IN THE SCHOOL'S PARKING lot when Curtis and Frankie pulled up. Matt and Joe had returned to their duties as patrol officers.

Monica was leaning against their car with her hands in her pockets.

Trevor stood a few feet away, speaking with an elderly woman with dyed blonde hair and a somber expression. Their conversation tapered off when Curtis and Frankie approached.

The woman was introduced as Annabeth Templeton, the principal of Blind River High School.

"I remember you," said Curtis. "You taught me chemistry back when you were a teacher."

"Yes," she said with a smile. "I'm impressed with what you've managed to accomplish, Curtis. I'm sure you'll be a source of inspiration for the students. I only wish you were coming back under better circumstances."

"You and I both." He introduced Frankie to Templeton. "Have you spoken to the friends of the missing girls?"

"They'll be waiting for you after your speech."

"Are they ready now?" said Curtis.

"You'll be speaking in the gym in about fifteen minutes. There are a lot of parents who've come to see the speech as well. I'll get you set up."

Curtis, Frankie, and the detectives followed her toward the school.

Frankie explained, "We want to make sure everyone is staying safe and isn't afraid to come forward with information. We need to know every dirty little secret Blind River has. You'd be amazed at the things that can blow a case wide open."

"I'm sure the students will do anything they can to help," said Templeton.

They walked into the gym. A microphone was set up at the front. Hundreds of eyes followed them as they walked through the center of the audience. Frankie scrunched up her shoulders.

Curtis took the mic and gave the speech they had worked out on the way over.

The students listened but fidgeted. Curtis listed what they could do to avoid danger, from always walking in pairs to making sure to avoid unpopulated or empty areas. The forest, in particular, was to be avoided. He spoke about the need to come to the police with any suspicions. He finished strong, promising that with their help he and Frankie would bring the girls home.

There was polite scattered applause, started by Principal Templeton. The students and parents seemed uncertain whether it was appropriate to clap.

Curtis thanked the crowd, and they walked back through

the center. Frankie scanned the audience, looking for anything that looked out of place. Nothing stood out.

A man with blond hair and a red collared shirt tight over his muscles approached them. He walked straight for Curtis, who stepped forward and put out a hand.

"Jeff Parker," said Curtis. "I'm surprised you're still in Blind River. I'd have thought you would have left."

"I did," said Jeff, not letting go of Curtis's hand and holding his gaze. "I came back when I realized there was nothing out there for me. I'm teaching math here, now."

Curtis grinned. "I'd expect nothing less."

"Good luck finding those girls," said Jeff, releasing Curtis's hand and turning around, joining the students who were leaving the gym.

Frankie turned to Curtis.

"Who was that?" she said.

"Jeff Parker," said Curtis under his breath. "A long time ago he was my best friend."

"What happened?"

Curtis looked around. "I found out he'd been working for Marino."

Frankie shot a look at Jeff's receding form. "What do you mean?"

"He worked for him when he was ten or eleven. He sold drugs. He was a minor, so he got off. That just makes it worse."

"Do you think he's involved with the case?"

"He might be a problem even if he isn't," said Curtis. "We need to keep an eye on him."

"You think he might be the kidnapper?"

Curtis considered it for a moment, then shook his head.

"Can't imagine it. He's too smart, and he would have no motive. We can put him on the list, but he isn't a kidnapper."

Monica and Trevor approached with Templeton, who led them to a classroom.

The students in the room were divided into four groups, all easily associated with one of the four missing girls. None of them seemed to have any connections to any of the other groups.

"Thank you all for coming," said Principal Templeton. The students looked up at the principal, the detectives, and two FBI agents. "You've all spoken with Detectives Mackley and Marshall, but these FBI agents need some time from you as well."

The detectives stayed in the classroom while Curtis and Frankie were brought to an adjacent office. The students were brought in one at a time.

With each student, Curtis and Frankie went through the statement they had made with Monica and Trevor, looking for inconsistencies or something recently remembered. Most, but not all, of the students had been with their missing friends the day they disappeared, and none had seen anything suspicious.

A few hours later, just as the clock struck three and Curtis realized he'd eaten nothing but a muffin the entire day, they finished their interviews.

Frankie leaned back in her chair as the last student left the room with Templeton.

"Anything?" said Curtis.

"No," said Frankie, picking up her notepad. It was covered with useless notes. "I thought I had something a few times, but there's always one victim who doesn't fit the theory. Two were mad at their parents, three were drinking the night before, two have after-school jobs, two were in relationships, none of them, allegedly, are doing any drugs, and only two use internet chat rooms. They don't have the same classes, social groups, or after-school activities. None of their parents are friends or even acquaintances. I don't think we're any closer than we were before."

Curtis ran his hands through his hair. "Without another kidnapping, we might never catch this guy. There are too many potential suspects. The butterfly hairclip from Miranda O'Connell doesn't have any prints on it, not even any signs of a struggle. It's a useless breadcrumb."

Frankie sighed. "We need someone else to get grabbed."

"Or the killer turns himself in."

"I'm trying to be realistic here, Curtis."

"Stranger things have happened."

There was a knock on the door, and Frankie told them to come in.

Principal Templeton entered with a boy who looked to be among the older grades in the school. Templeton stood with one hand on the boy's shoulder and said, "Zach would like to speak with you."

"Great," said Curtis. "Come on in, Zach. Take a seat."

Zach, a lanky boy who looked like a computer programmer, took his seat. He glanced behind him and waited until Principal Templeton had closed the door before he turned back to the agents.

"What is it?" said Frankie. "You knew one of the victims?"

"Yeah," said Zach. His posture was relaxed, but he looked as though he'd been trying to gather up the bravery to come and speak with them, and now that he was in the home stretch he was beginning to have second thoughts. He took a deep breath and said, "It's about Ashley."

"Ashley Hagerty? What about her?"

Zach looked up at them through his bangs and shrugged. "Well, we were dating."

Curtis and Frankie paused for a moment.

"You were?" said Curtis. "How did that happen? No offense, but you don't seem like the type of guy she'd normally be going out with."

Zach nodded. "I know. I live down the street from her. We've known each other since we were little kids, but it wasn't until recently we started hanging out again. She didn't want anyone to know, which I was fine with. That's her business. I just wanted to spend time with her. When she disappeared, I didn't know what to do. No one knew what had happened. No one knew we were going out."

Frankie nodded. "Thank you so much for coming to speak with us. We promise this won't get out unless you want it to, or if it becomes crucial to find her."

"Thanks." Zach glanced over his shoulder, then back at them.

Curtis said, "Is there anything that you can think of in the days leading up to Ashley's disappearance?"

"No." He shook his head. "I've thought about it a lot. She had her school and her friends. She spends a lot of time at the gym, maybe people there saw something. I talked to her on the phone, but I didn't spend any significant time with her over the last few days. I miss her so much." He trailed off, staring at the floor.

Frankie took a card from the inside of her jacket and

passed it across the table. "If you think of anything," she said, "let us know."

Zach nodded and took the card, looking at it for a moment, then sliding it into his pocket. "I will. Thank you." He stood and walked to the door, then out into the hallway.

Templeton leaned in. Frankie told her to send the detectives in.

A minute later, Monica and Trevor walked into the room and took the two seats across from them. Frankie brought them up to speed, essentially declaring they knew a lot more while not having learned anything useful.

"What about Zach?" said Trevor. "You think he's worth investigating?"

Frankie shrugged. "Open a file on him and see if there's anything in his past which would indicate deviant behavior, but I can't see it."

Curtis nodded. "The only possible motive he could have was anger that Ashley wouldn't tell anyone they were dating, but that doesn't explain the other kidnappings."

Monica checked her phone. "You two have a package from the FBI offices waiting for you. We've also got the list of suspects in the area finished. Want to head back to the station?"

"We'll meet you there," said Curtis.

Monica raised an eyebrow. "Sure?"

"Yeah, I'll see you there."

Monica shrugged and stood, followed by Trevor.

Once they were gone, Frankie turned to Curtis and said, "You aren't going to tell her about Marino and Bobby Randall? What if it comes up later in the investigation?"

"It isn't important. Monica will just get concerned. What did Johnson say?"

Frankie paused. "He just wanted to know how you were dealing, and if I suspected anything. If I did, he wants me to call him, and he'll pull us out."

"That's it? What did you say about me?"

"I said you were fine." She stood. "Come on, let's go. I'll drop you off at the bar to speak with Bobby Randall. I need to speak with Natasha Nolowinski."

"Is that what Kendra Matheson was telling you, or is that just based on the article?"

"Both," said Frankie. "If Natasha knows something, she can't keep holding it for herself, and we need to stop the leaks from the police department."

CHAPTER 21

CURTIS STEPPED INSIDE THE BAR. HIS STOMACH WAS GROWLING. He was thankful when Robert walked toward him, wearing the same jolly smile as always.

"Curtis!" he said with a shout, which caused the rest of the bar to look up before returning to their drinks. "How you doing, lad? It's so great to see you again. How's the investigation doing? What can I do for you?"

"I'm actually here in connection to the investigation," said Curtis as he took a seat at the bar. "Is Bobby here?"

Robert's smile vanished. "Yeah, I'll grab him for you. Want anything to drink or eat?"

"Water and a burger would be great."

"Sure, you want fries?"

"Yes, please."

"Why don't you have a seat at one of the tables and I'll send him out with your food in a few?"

Robert got him a glass of water, then turned and walked away, speaking with a few of his regulars before disappearing into the kitchen.

Curtis grabbed the glass and walked over to an empty table. He leaned back in his seat, watching the pool balls bounce around the table as two men dragged the game on longer than any pool game should go.

Bobby emerged from the kitchen with a serious expression, carrying a tray laden with food. He dropped off a few plates at other tables before arriving with Curtis's burger and fries. He placed it on the table and took a seat opposite Curtis.

"So," said Bobby. "How did it go with Marino? You went and saw him, right?"

"I went and saw him," said Curtis between bites of the overcooked burger. "He didn't seem like he had any animosity toward me. He didn't seem to know anything about the girls, and he certainly didn't seem like he wanted to kill me. What are your thoughts on that?"

Bobby shrugged. "That's odd. It goes against everything I'd heard."

Curtis placed the burger on the plate and looked up at Bobby. "Tell me everything about your stay in prison."

Bobby hesitated for a moment before nodding. "I suppose I have to tell you, with you being the FBI and everything."

Curtis didn't respond. He had no right to force Bobby to tell him anything without a warrant, especially since he had no probable cause that his information would be related to the missing girls. In all probability, it would have nothing to do with the missing girls, but was instead information for Curtis's own safety in Blind River.

"I was sentenced to six months for a variety of small crimes that piled up," said Bobby. "I'm sure you've already read that in my file. Some of that stuff had to do with Marino."

Curtis hadn't, but he nodded.

"I wasn't able to hold down any jobs, and I got involved in some bad stuff," said Bobby. "My parents went to Florida for my mom's cancer treatment. I could never afford to visit her. I needed to stay and make money. I took the easy route, got involved with some criminal types. Some bigwigs are still using the systems that Marino set up to traffic drugs, using Blind River as a waypoint."

He was giving information Curtis didn't know and wasn't in the FBI's files, but Curtis wasn't about to stop him. Bobby was speaking as though he needed to get this off his chest.

Curtis glanced at Robert standing behind the bar, who smiled back in that grandfatherly way he had.

Bobby continued, "There are people in town who are still keeping Marino's network alive, trying to continue his work. I don't know how many of them there are, but me and a few others all got caught with it. I was given six months. The warden wouldn't let me out for my mom's funeral. My dad threw a fit over it. He ended up fighting one of the prison guards, a guy named Harry Ochre. My dad's not a fighter, but he's a big guy. I'd never seen that side of him. He was arrested for it, but the guard decided not to press charges. It didn't help my case. I got out in five months for good behavior, but I only ever got to see my mom's gravestone."

Bobby stared at the table. "Sorry, what were you asking about?"

"Marino, in the prison," said Curtis.

"Right, sorry. It just feels good to talk, you know."

"I know."

"Marino was there," said Bobby. "I never talked to him. He and his cronies had one corner of the yard under their control, and one of the first things I learned was to stay away from Marino."

"He controlled the prison?"

"Still does, from what I heard," said Bobby. "The other thing I heard while I was there is that he was looking for Curtis Mackley, an FBI agent. I walked past his cell one time. He had a dart board in there. He could get whatever he wanted, although the dart board was one of those magnetic ones, nothing sharp for obvious reasons. There was a picture of you on it. It looked like it was printed from the FBI website."

Curtis raised an eyebrow. "Really?"

Bobby nodded.

"Can you prove it? That sounds ridiculous."

"What do you mean can I prove it? I saw it."

Curtis dipped a fry into his ketchup. "Did you?"

Bobby bit his lip then shook his head. "No, I'm sorry. I heard about it. I didn't see it. I might have misheard. I know he was looking for you, and you said you didn't think he was. I swear to God, he has it out for you."

Curtis picked up one of his fries and chewed it. "Are you sure? What did he say he would do?"

Bobby swallowed. "He said he would hang you from the rafters and gut you like the hogs in his butcher shop."

"That's pleasant," said Curtis. "Thank you, Bobby. I appreciate you telling me what you heard. I'll be back if I need to ask you anything else."

"Thanks," Bobby stood. "You'll save those girls, right?"

Curtis nodded, trying to look more confident than he felt. "We'll find them. I wish you the best of luck in the future."

"Thanks," said Bobby, showing the first smile Curtis had seen on him. He turned and walked back to the bar.

Curtis was left sitting at the table alone. He lifted up the overcooked burger and took a big bite. He was hungry enough that he wasn't going to be too picky.

CHAPTER 22

FRANKIE PARKED OUTSIDE THE OFFICES OF THE BLIND RIVER Observer. The spot reserved for Natasha Nolowinski had a blue car sitting in it. The front desk was unmanned, and Frankie walked right into the offices.

"Excuse me," shouted one of the reporters. "You aren't allowed back here. Someone has to escort you."

"FBI," she said, flashing her badge. "Where's Natasha Nolowinski?"

The man, phone still held to his ear, looking frightened, pointed to the far side of the office. Frankie nodded to him before heading in that direction.

Natasha was sitting at her desk, wearing a large pair of headphones and typing away at her computer. Her desk was cluttered with notes. Boston Red Sox bobbleheads lined the top of the cubicle wall.

Frankie leaned over the wall and looked down at Natasha, who was typing and chewing on a pen.

Frankie reached down and waved a hand in front of Natasha's face. It was only then that she looked up at Frankie.

Natasha smiled and removed her headphones. She removed the pen from her mouth, one end chewed almost to the ink and placed it on the desk. "What can I do you for, Agent?"

"You need to tell me two things right now," said Frankie. "Who are you getting your information from? And two, what do you know about the missing girls? Withholding information about the girls' whereabouts can be construed as obstructing an investigation."

Natasha smirked. "One, I don't have to tell you the name of my source. That would be against journalistic ethics, and I would never get a job again. As to knowing something about the investigation, whoever told you that is full of shit. You can look through my notes if you want. You won't find anything about my source."

"How about we cut the shit, Natasha?" Frankie came around the desk and stood close to her. "You don't care about journalistic ethics. If you did, you wouldn't have written that article in the Observer this morning about how Agent Mackley is obsessed with Marino."

Natasha shrugged. "I'll be happy to mention that in tomorrow's paper."

Frankie frowned. "Let me see your notes."

Natasha handed over the notebook from her desk. As she did so, she brushed past Frankie's jacket. "This is nice fabric," she said.

Frankie shoved her aside, barely retaining her composure. "I'm taking this as evidence," said Frankie. "I expect a full retraction in tomorrow's Observer, along with a full vote of confidence from the Observer in both the Blind River

Police Department and the FBI. Anything less and I'll be back here with a warrant. Understood?"

"Understood."

"Good." Frankie stared at Natasha for a moment before turning and walking out of the office.

As she was about to leave, she looked back at Natasha, feeling uneasy about trusting anything she said.

CHAPTER 23

CURTIS WAITED OUTSIDE THE BAR TO BE PICKED UP BY FRANKIE. They would be heading to the station to update Chief Tucker before going to the Blind River Motel, where they had rooms booked for the night.

Taking advantage of the downtime, he took out his phone and dialed Melanie.

She answered on the second ring. "Hello?"

"Hey, Mel."

"Oh, hey, Curtis. I wasn't expecting to hear from you today."

"Nothing was going on so I thought I'd check in."

There was a pause. "Morning sickness is getting worse. I haven't been able to get as much work done. On the bright side, today was the first time I got offered a seat on the subway."

Curtis laughed. "That's awesome. How did they like those sketches for the Ford advertisement?"

"They seemed to like them. I just got out of the meeting

with the sales team, actually. I'm waiting to hear back from them."

"Good luck. How's the baby?"

"He kicked this morning."

"Really?"

"Yeah, it felt weird, but also great, you know?"

"I wish I was there."

"You'll be here for the next first."

"I'll be back." He felt a lump form in his throat as he remembered making the same promise to Amber. "I promised. I'll be back as soon as I can."

"How's the case?"

"I don't know. I wish I hadn't come back here."

"Then come back to me, Curtis."

He looked up. Frankie turned the corner toward him.

"There are some questions I need answers to," he said. "Then I'll be back, I promise."

"Okay. Be safe."

The line went dead just as Frankie pulled up.

He worried for a moment, after the promises he'd broken before, whether his promises meant anything.

CHAPTER 24

CURTIS WAS JOLTED OUT OF HIS SLEEP BY A SUDDEN ONSLAUGHT of light.

It was still dark outside. The clock on the bedside table said it was just past four in the morning. Frankie had still been awake when Curtis had fallen asleep. She'd been going through Natasha's notes.

"What the hell?" said Curtis, looking up at Frankie standing over his bed. The lights in the room had all been switched on. "For fuck's sake, can't I just have a normal night's sleep for one night?"

"Zach O'Reilly's missing," said Frankie.

Curtis looked up at her, frowning.

"What?" he said.

"He never came home after he spoke to us about Ashley," said Frankie. "His parents called the cops. They can't find any trace of him."

"Jesus Christ." Curtis pushed himself onto his elbows. "Okay, give me a minute to have a shower and get dressed."

Ten minutes later, they were driving through the empty town. They pulled up to the O'Reilly's house.

Matt Oberman was standing by his car. They parked and walked up. The house was completely surrounded by police cars and yellow tape, the flashing lights from the cars illuminating the street.

The neighbors leaned out of their doors to see what was happening, their expressions a mix of sorrow and relief it wasn't their family. Just a few blocks down the street was the Hagertys' residence, where they had interviewed Miriam and Ken two days earlier.

Curtis and Frankie walked up to Matt. He looked up as they approached.

"What happened?" said Curtis.

Matt shrugged. "Mr. and Mrs. O'Reilly called the police at around midnight when Zach hadn't come home. We've gotten a ton of calls like that since the kidnappings started, but we sent a squad car out to check on it. The officer found a significant amount of blood in the back garden, so we got called in."

"Zach was here last night," said Frankie.

Matt nodded. "The parents were out at a movie."

"This isn't the same guy," said Frankie.

"What do you mean?" said Matt, frowning.

"It's not the same person who kidnapped the girls. It's too far from his M.O. It's too messy and too risky. Why would he do it?"

"You're saying there's someone else?"

"It makes more sense than saying it was the same person."

Curtis nodded. "Our guy is kidnapping girls, specifically

targeted from separate social groups and taken in the middle of the night, in deserted areas where no one can see them. This is too barbaric, too simplistic."

"Maybe he's changing it up?" said Matt. "We don't exactly have a big sample size."

"Unlikely," said Frankie. "There's something about those girls that the kidnapper is focusing on. It just doesn't make sense."

Matt nodded and turned back toward the house. Through the front door, they could see two officers speaking with the O'Reilly's. Zach's mother sobbed while her husband held her close, barely holding himself together.

"Get them to look for footprints," said Curtis. He and Frankie turned and walked back toward their car.

"Where are you going?" said Oberman.

Frankie answered. "This isn't our case. It might be related, but it's something else. Make sure the detectives get us the information."

They got to their car just as Monica and Trevor pulled up. Monica nodded to Curtis, and he nodded back.

Curtis climbed into the car.

"We've got a few hours until your meeting with Marino," said Frankie as she pulled away from the flurry of police activity. "Let's check out the forest again."

"Are you thinking that's the dumping ground?"

"If the kidnapper is killing the girls, it makes sense to take the bodies out to the forest and bury them."

"The police checked that. It was in the file. They had a full team from the State Police come in and take dogs through the forest."

"Just because they didn't find anything doesn't mean that there isn't something to be found."

Curtis looked over at Frankie. She had that expression which he'd seen so many times before. Marino was his crusade, this was hers.

He nodded.

They pulled into the same parking lot they'd visited after their arrival, just as the first rays of sun appeared over the lake.

Walking along the edge of the forest, they came to the spot where they believed Harriet Matheson had been grabbed. Curtis stared into the forest and frowned. Something was bothering him, a faint, almost forgotten memory pushing at the edges of his mind.

A squirrel ran along the branches above them. Birds flew between the trees, chirping happily.

Frankie stared into the forest, then began walking. She took out a flashlight and began scanning the ground, looking for anything that might indicate a buried body. Curtis did the same.

They searched for two hours. The sunlight reached between the trees.

Without speaking a word, they turned and made their way back toward town, retracing the same steps.

Curtis knew they had long ago passed the point that a body would be buried by all except the strongest, most determined serial killer.

When they got back to the river, Frankie turned and looked at the forest, as if demanding to know its secrets.

Frankie twisted her mouth into a scowl.

"Anything?" said Curtis, his hands in his pockets.

"No," said Frankie. "Let's go into the station. Maybe they know what happened to Zach. We can pick up the evidence for Marino."

CHAPTER 25

THE COMMOTION FROM THE O'REILLYS' HOUSE HAD MOVED TO the police station. Cars, both police, and civilian filled the street.

There was a mob gathered at the entrance, shouting at the few police officers, among whom was Joe Hagerty, that they wanted answers.

"Our children are being taken by a madman!" screamed someone.

"The police are useless!" another shouted.

There was a camera flash, and the voice of Natasha Nolowinski came over the crowd. She shouted, "Officers, what do you have to say about allegations of bribery and incompetence?"

The answer was drowned out by the shouting. Curtis and Frankie ducked their heads as they drove past and parked two blocks from the station.

They walked back to the police station, trying to sneak around to the back entrance. They were halfway around the building when Natasha Nolowinski shouted, "There are the

FBI agents! They aren't even trying to find the girls! They're just trying to satisfy their own revenge!"

Parents and teachers Curtis recognized, among many others, began marching toward them.

Curtis and Frankie jogged through the back doors of the station. They locked the door and looked around the interior of the station.

"I'm getting a warrant for Nolowinski," muttered Frankie through her teeth. "I don't care what it's for." She turned to the nearest officer and said, "Where are Mackley and Marshall?"

The officer pointed to the chief's office.

Frankie and Curtis entered the office without knocking. Monica and Trevor waited patiently while the chief shouted into his phone to someone about the mob outside the station. He glanced at them for just a moment.

"They're here now," said the chief. "I'll tell them. Okay, thank you." He slammed the phone into its cradle and let out three heaving breaths. He looked up at the agents and the detectives. "That was the mayor," he said. "She wants to know why bringing in the FBI has made the situation worse."

Frankie frowned. "We—"

"I know," said Tucker, falling into his chair and adjusting his tie. "It's only been two days. People in this town have this mystical fucking view of the FBI."

"What's going on?" said Frankie. "Why is there a mob out there?"

Tucker sighed. "I assume you haven't seen today's Observer." He reached into the drawer and pulled out a newspaper.

Curtis took it. His stomach sank as he saw Zach's picture

plastered over the front page. The headline said, "Secret boyfriend of missing girl questioned by police."

The article was written by Natasha Nolowinski. Two things became apparent as Curtis read the article. One, the article implied Zach was the only suspect, and two, nowhere in the article did it explicitly say that.

Curtis understood and sighed. "Someone read this and decided to take justice into their own hands?"

"Not just someone," said Trevor, leaning forward with his elbows on his knees. "Ken Hagerty."

Curtis frowned. "Ashley's dad?"

Trevor nodded. "Neighbors saw him grab Zach from the O'Reillys' backyard. Baseball bat to the head knocked the kid out. Ken threw Zach over his shoulder and walked to his car. Threw Zach into the trunk and drove off."

"So," said Chief Tucker, "what do we do? This is so far outside my area of expertise, I don't even know where to begin. I never thought I'd be dealing with this kind of situation here. I'm not prepared for this." The chief laughed to himself. "A few months ago, Natasha was in here harassing me about a comment I made regarding a fight at Randall's Tavern where a guy got his teeth knocked out. I thought the backlash from that article would be the lowest point of my career. I told myself if I got through that, I'd be fine." Chief Tucker looked out through the window. At that moment, he looked like a man who was tired of everything.

"We need to divide and conquer," said Frankie. "We should put one FBI agent with one detective to make sure we have a combination of expertise and local knowledge. Curtis and Monica will focus on finding the missing girls. Trevor and I will find Ken Hagerty. Any questions?"

Curtis met Monica's gaze. She stared right back at him, her expression unreadable. No one asked any questions.

"Let's get to it," said Frankie, "before something else happens."

Curtis grabbed the box of FBI evidence from the corner of the office.

They left Chief Tucker white-knuckling the edge of his desk, his forehead turning a bright red as his phone rang.

They walked through the screaming crowds once again, ignoring them. Natasha was standing near the outside of the crowd, grinning at them.

Monica and Trevor's detective car was parked along the side of the road, the mob blocking any of the reserved parking spots. Curtis and Monica climbed into the police car. Curtis put the box of evidence in the footwell of the back seat. Frankie and Trevor walked to the FBI car. They drove in opposite directions.

"Where to?" said Monica from the driver's seat. "I want to drop by dad's house at some point."

"Just drive around for a bit," said Curtis. "I want to make sure we aren't being followed."

"And then?"

"We'll go to the prison."

They drove for a few minutes, Curtis looking out the back windshield. When he was sure they weren't being followed, he told Monica to drive to the prison.

"You really think Marino has something to do with this?" said Monica. "There's no reason Marino would want to kidnap a bunch of girls. This isn't about you and him, Curtis."

"Did you know?" said Curtis. "That it was me who put Marino in prison?"

Monica nodded. "I thought it might be you, but couldn't prove it. I asked Condra about a month before he died. He said it was a very good guess and sipped his whiskey."

"So dad didn't know?" said Curtis.

"I don't think so."

Curtis nodded and stared out the window as the rows of houses gave way to trees and transport trucks passing by on the highway, the prison looming in the distance.

"Marino knows," he said.

"Are you sure?"

"He figured it out when he found out I was in the FBI. It's not a huge logical leap that the kid who delivered his paper turned him in, especially if that kid winds up in the FBI."

"Where'd you get that information?"

"Bobby Randall."

Monica scoffed. "Bobby Randall was a low-level drug dealer who got caught because he sold crack to a cop. Not an undercover cop. A uniformed patrol cop in his patrol car. Bobby is a moron."

Curtis frowned. "Bobby said he heard it while in prison. He didn't say anything about drug dealing."

"Don't trust him, Curtis," said Monica. "His own father doesn't trust him alone at the bar, and any delusion he has about inheriting the bar is never going to happen."

They pulled into the parking lot of the prison. Curtis wondered whether there were more useful things they could be doing. They climbed out of the car. Curtis grabbed the evidence box from the back seat.

Nate Williams looked up from his desk as they approached. He stared at Monica for a moment, then turned to Curtis, ignoring Monica.

Monica said nothing but visibly tensed up her shoulders. Curtis wondered whether they'd talked since the divorce.

"What can I do for you, Agent?" said Nate.

"I need to speak with Marino again."

Nate nodded and called up to the prison. He spoke to someone on the other side, then hung up. "Harry will meet you inside," he said.

Curtis thanked him and walked inside. Monica didn't acknowledge Nate as she followed.

"What happened between you and Nate?" said Curtis as they walked toward the interview rooms.

"When did you get married?" said Monica abruptly.

Curtis stopped. The evidence box weighed down his arms.

Monica walked a few steps ahead before realizing Curtis had stopped. It was the first time he'd been alone with his sister in almost fifteen years. He thought of the ring in his pocket, where he had kept it since taking it off.

"What are you waiting for?" she said. "Trevor and I both saw your wedding ring. Get over it."

She continued walking down the hall. After a few moments, Curtis followed.

At the end of the hallway, they were met by Harry Ochre. He led them to an interview room.

Monica stayed outside to watch through the one-way mirror while Curtis entered.

Curtis placed the evidence box on the ground and took a seat.

Marino entered from the other side of the room, flanked by guards Curtis didn't know. He smiled at Curtis as his handcuffs were attached to the table.

Neither said anything until the guards left the room.

"So," said Marino, "how's the investigation?"

"It's going well," said Curtis. "We're set to make an arrest later today."

"Are you?" Marino raised an eyebrow. "Who are you arresting? It's about time you morons started catching up."

"That's confidential."

"The answer to any question an FBI agent doesn't like." Marino leaned back in his chair and grinned. "You should start listening to me, Curtis. This town is more mine than yours. I lived here for forty years. For about ten years I was, for all intents and purposes, the judge, jury, and executioner. Those are my people out there. I want to help, but I have to look out for myself first. I know who's killing those girls, but I need something in return."

"How's this?" Curtis took a folder from the box. He slid it across the table to Marino, who picked it up with his cuffed hands and began flipping through.

Marino read the folder front to back, then placed it on the desk. He looked up at Curtis. "This is fake."

"It's real," said Curtis. "I have assurance from the FBI that this is valid intel."

Marino shrugged. "It's fake."

"Which parts?" said Curtis. "It could be beneficial to the FBI if there are errors in our information."

Marino laughed. "If you won't respect me, I'd like to go back to my cell now."

"Sam, you have to listen to me." Curtis leaned in. "There are lives at risk."

The guards came into the room. Marino stood as his cuffs were unattached from the table. He looked at the one-way mirror. "Does your partner know what this is really about?"

Curtis glanced at the mirror. It took a moment to realize that Marino thought Frankie was behind the glass.

"What are you talking about?" said Curtis.

"Your brother, Josh. For the right price, I'll tell you how he died." He grinned.

Curtis remembered what Bobby Randall had told him about Marino putting a price on his head.

"What do you know?" Curtis said through gritted teeth.

Marino laughed and turned to the guards. "I want to go back to my cell."

The guards looked at Curtis.

"Take him away," said Curtis. "He's bluffing. We'll talk when he's ready to be serious."

Marino was led from the interview room without looking back.

Once the door closed, Curtis sat for a moment before picking up the box of useless evidence. He walked out of the room.

Outside, Monica was still looking through the mirror. Harry stood a few feet away.

"Is it true?" said Monica. "What he said about Josh?"

"No," said Curtis. "He's full of it."

Harry led them back to Nate, who led them to their car. Curtis put the box of evidence in the back seat and climbed into the passenger seat.

"Where to?" said Monica in a professional manner once they had passed through the gates.

"Crime scenes," said Curtis. "I want to walk through them again. There must be some similarity between the crime scenes, something that was going through the kidnapper's head when he selected his victims, and the places he would grab them, even if he didn't realize it."

Monica was silent for a moment, then said, "We never spoke about Josh. I was too young when he disappeared to understand."

Curtis stared out the window. "It's complicated."

Monica pulled into the parking lot of a coffee shop. "I deserve to know, especially if it's important."

"We need to get to the crime scenes," said Curtis.

"Five minutes won't make a difference."

"You never asked Dad?"

Monica sighed. "I tried, but he never wanted to talk about it. Once he started losing his memory, he started talking about Josh as though he was still there, but it was jumbled, and I was never able to distinguish what was real."

"I can't tell you exactly," said Curtis. "I don't know all the details. I was twelve. Josh and Dad tried to make us believe everything was fine. Josh dropped out of the police academy. He and Dad got into a fight about it. Josh stormed off and didn't come home until four in the morning. I stayed up until I was sure he was home. Within a few weeks, Dad kicked him out of the house. He didn't say why, just that Josh wouldn't be living with us anymore. I think Josh had started working with Marino. A few more weeks after that, Dad told me Josh had moved away, and he wouldn't be back. It didn't take long for the other kids at school to tell me the rumors that he was missing and might have been killed. There was no proof. We received no letters, no calls, nothing to indicate that he was alive or dead. I always assumed he was dead. It's easier that way."

"So what?" said Monica after a pause. "That's it?"

"I searched for him on the FBI database. They had a file on him as a suspected associate of Marino. He's been declared legally dead. There's nothing to indicate he's alive."

"But he could be?"

"I don't know." Curtis looked around the parking lot. "I just don't know. Come on, let's visit the crime scenes."

Monica looked as though she was going to ask a question, then said nothing. She turned on the car and drove out of the parking lot.

CHAPTER 26

MIRIAM HAGERTY WAS CRYING AGAIN. TO FRANKIE, IT SEEMED like the only thing she did. Neither she nor Trevor was any good at calming her down without letting their own emotions and irritation get out of hand.

Trevor was crouching in front of Miriam with his hand on her shoulder, saying all the right things, but without any of the genuine caring Curtis was able to conjure up at a moment's notice.

Eventually, Miriam stopped crying, although it seemed she had simply run out of tears to cry.

"Miriam," said Frankie, sitting on the couch across from her and doing a poor job containing her irritation, "what happened last night? We need to know everything if we're going to save Zach's life."

Miriam let out a wail. Frankie braced herself for another round of tears, but it never came.

Instead, Miriam said, in a completely level tone, "Ken has never liked feeling helpless. He once told me that nothing could harm him in life if he could control it. All this stuff with

Ashley, and that's probably someone we see every day who took her, was too much for him. Ken couldn't save his daughter."

"What about Zach?" Trevor said. Frankie put a hand on his arm to stop him from talking.

"All the news about it has been hard." Miriam looked to one side, avoiding their eyes. "I haven't been sleeping. Ken only sleeps after he's had a few drinks. I stay up waiting for a phone call from Ashley or a police officer telling us something. Last night, there was a call around one in the morning. Ken was still down here, drinking. He answered on the second ring. I came downstairs, my heart fluttering, hoping it was about Ashley. Ken was asking who the caller was, then he thanked them and hung up. He barged past me and grabbed his coat. I asked him what he was doing, and he said a reporter had called for a comment on Zach O'Reilly." Miriam took a deep breath, looking relieved to have shared the story with someone.

"What happened next?" said Frankie.

"He left the house without another word," said Miriam. "The next thing I heard about it was the sirens at the O'Reilly's place. I don't see how Zach could have done it. He seemed like such a kind and caring boy, but if Ashley wasn't telling us she was seeing him, then maybe there is something. Did Zach kill my daughter?"

"No," said Frankie. "I don't believe Zach had anything to do with it. We've investigated him. There's nothing to link him to the crimes. The reporter was falsely informed. Speaking of which, do you know who the reporter was?"

"It sounded like a woman."

Frankie made a mental note to speak with Natasha

Nolowinski. "If Ken were to hide somewhere," she said, "where would he go?"

Miriam thought for a moment. "He works in construction. A lot of the houses he works on are within an hour from here. Probably one of those. I've wondered a few times if he brought other women to those houses before the owners moved in."

"Do you have the addresses?"

Miriam swallowed. "What are you going to do if you catch him?"

"We're going to arrest him," said Frankie flatly. "We're going to charge him with kidnapping at the minimum. Depending on Zach's state, we might charge him with something else. Think about Mr. and Mrs. O'Reilly. They want their son back, just like you want Ashley back."

"Do you have children, Agent?"

"No."

"I thought you might." Miriam turned to look at the wall, as though she could see the O'Reillys' house a few properties down. "Detective Marshall," she said, "can I borrow a page from your notepad? I'll tell you about the properties I know of."

"Thank you," said Frankie.

Trevor tore out a page from his notebook and handed it to Miriam, along with a pen.

"I'm not doing it for you," said Miriam. "I'm doing it for Ashley."

"What do you mean?" said Frankie.

She turned back to them. "If Ashley loved Zach, I'll do what I can to protect him, no matter what Ken or I think of him."

CHAPTER 27

CURTIS CROUCHED AND LOOKED OVER THE THIRD CRIME SCENE. He looked both ways down the street. There was a park in front of him and houses in every other direction.

"Miranda O'Connell was taken here?" he said.

"About ten feet that way is our best guess," said Monica, pointing to the right.

Curtis stood and walked to the spot. "The butterfly hairclip was here?"

Monica nodded. She was leaning against the car and giving her serious cop gaze to anyone who wandered too close. It was a look their father had always used when they were young.

"This is interesting," said Curtis. "This is the only disappearance we can peg to an exact location. All the others were grabbed somewhere within a larger area, and we can only guess at specifics. If you were going to kidnap someone from this area, why pick this spot? What's special about here?"

Monica shrugged. "There aren't many windows that face

this area. There are porches, but it was late at night. No one would be looking at the park."

"Maybe the kidnapper lives around here," said Curtis. "This is the highest risk area, and it isn't close."

"Maybe it was about Miranda O'Connell," said Monica. "She was important enough that he was willing to take a risk."

Curtis considered it. "It's possible. It's not uncommon for serial killers and kidnappers to target people who remind them of someone from their past. Does Miranda O'Connell have any siblings?"

"You spoke with her parents. You should know that."

"I haven't been here in a long time. Being the only child at home doesn't mean she was the only child."

"As far as I'm aware, she's her parents' only child."

"What about the parents?" said Curtis. "Anything in her past that would indicate connections with unruly people? Maybe Marino's people?"

"I'll check. How is the FBI helpline doing?"

Curtis let out a long sigh. "I hate those things. They make all the junior agents spend some time manning the phones just to get an appreciation for how mind-numbing it is. For every thousand tips you get, there might be one that's useful."

"So nothing?"

"Nothing worth investigating." Curtis kicked at a small rock. "We have teams at the New York office investigating the validity of all the calls. Most will be people trying to get the prize money and have their fifteen minutes of fame. We'll keep checking, but Director Johnson will pull the plug on it eventually."

Monica nodded, then looked up and frowned. "What if it's because this spot isn't under any streetlights?"

Curtis followed where she was looking. There was an irregular spacing between the streetlights, instead of the normal blanket covering. The space they were standing in was at thirty feet from streetlights on all sides. If it were night, they would be in complete darkness.

"If a car rolled up here," said Curtis, "and Miranda recognized the driver, and he offered her a ride, then that could be the answer."

"Why would she have dropped her hair clip?"

"By accident?" said Curtis. "Maybe she was doing her hair, got distracted, was in a rush. It would explain why the kidnapper didn't pick it up. It would never occur to him that she'd dropped anything."

"How does that fit with the other girls?"

"They were all alone. A trusted authority figure drives up and asks if they want a drive. They get into the car, thinking it's nothing suspicious. Maybe he offers a spiked drink, or maybe he knocks them out once they're somewhere quiet."

"What about Harriet Matheson?" said Monica. "She was with her friends. Why would she have wanted to get in the car?"

"He could have offered to help buy the booze and cigarettes from the convenience store. Maybe the kidnapper offered to buy them for her, then give her a ride back to her friends."

"And the other two? Ashley and Darcy?"

"Same thing. He offers a ride home or to wherever they were going. He acts like he's being a good Samaritan. Maybe he says he would feel guilty if anything happened to them."

"So who would it be?" said Monica. "This is a small town. Saying it's a trusted person doesn't really narrow it down."

"We work backward from the last case. Harriet Matheson was kidnapped at a time when the normal small-town attitude of trusting everyone would be gone. She wouldn't intuitively trust anyone unless she knew them well. Ashley Hagerty was the first, and she would have taken a ride from anyone she recognized."

"So we start looking into Harriet's connections?"

"Yeah, although I still think we need to look for mutual acquaintances."

"How many people would four teenage girls from different social groups all know? We're basically narrowing it down to school teachers and public officials."

Curtis grimaced. There was something on the edge of his consciousness, a clue behind a locked door inside his mind.

"I know," he said. "We're missing something. This guy is smart. He would have figured this out. Let's go see the next crime scene."

Monica nodded and climbed into the driver's seat.

Her phone rang. She gave Curtis an apologetic look that turned to worry when she saw the caller ID. "I have to take this," she said.

She answered the phone and walked a dozen feet away. Curtis watched her posture shift from concern to panic, her volume rising as she spoke. She hung up, turned, and walked back to the car.

Inside the car, Curtis asked who it was.

"Dad's nurse." Monica started the car and pulled onto the street. "He had a stroke. An ambulance is taking him to the hospital."

Curtis stared at her for a moment as she pulled away from the curb. He leaned his head against the cold glass of the window.

At that moment, as Monica cheated a few speed limits, it occurred to him for the first time that his father, the man who had raised him, who had done his best as a father, who was the reason he'd gotten into law enforcement in the first place, might not live forever.

CHAPTER 28

FRANKIE AND TREVOR ARRIVED AT THE FIRST CONSTRUCTION
site on the list Miriam had given them. There was a thin layer
of dew built up over the frame. It was a three-story vacation
home on the lake.

They showed their badges to the security guard, who
claimed to have seen no one enter the house, and made no
effort to slow them down.

Trevor walked across the half-finished lawn and into the
empty doorway. The door itself lay a few feet away. Miriam
had claimed Ken didn't own any guns, that he was adamantly
anti-gun as a matter of fact. Frankie unclipped her holster
anyway. They moved through the living room, listening for
any indication they weren't alone.

Footprints zig-zagged across the floors from workers
who'd been there two days prior. There were no fresh
footprints.

They did a full circuit of the aboveground floors before
moving to the basement. It was dark and open concept, with
cinderblock walls and support beams. Frankie stepped off the

wooden staircase onto the dirt floor, scanning the basement with a large flashlight they'd brought from the car. Trevor followed a few steps behind.

The basement was empty, and a cursory search revealed no hidden spaces. When Frankie had done a full circuit, she returned to the staircase where Trevor was waiting. "He's not here," she said. "Let's move on."

As they left, the security guard grunted at them.

Trevor's phone rang as they approached the car. He walked a few steps away and answered. He listened and spoke for a few minutes before ending the call and returning to Frankie.

"That was Monica," he said. "Gordon Mackley was taken to the hospital. She and Curtis are with the doctors."

Frankie nodded. "How long are they going to be?"

Trevor turned and stared at her. "Their father could be dying. I didn't ask how long they were going to be."

"Those girls could be dying, too. Let's go." Frankie climbed into the driver's seat.

Trevor climbed in after her, fidgeting as he pulled the seatbelt across his body.

"Where are we going?" said Frankie.

Trevor hesitated, then said, "Go to the right."

CHAPTER 29

GORDON MACKLEY HAD BEEN ASLEEP FOR ALMOST FIVE HOURS. Monica and Curtis had been by his bedside during that time, waiting for him to wake up. The doctors had explained that he'd had a stroke.

His body was connected to a variety of beeping machines. It had initially annoyed Curtis but had since become a rhythm which brought him comfort that his father was still alive.

Curtis had taken breaks to listen to Frankie's reports about one construction site after another, yielding nothing as to Ken Hagerty's location.

Inside the room, Gordon Mackley began mumbling as the drugs wore off. The words were either nonsense or impossible to decipher, but Josh's name came up over and over again. It was the only name he mentioned.

Monica asked if Curtis wanted any food. He said he did. Monica left and headed to the cafeteria.

Once he was alone, Curtis looked out the window, thinking about the missing girls.

In his experience, all cases fell into one of two groups. Some cases were like this one, with a million clues and nothing pointing to an obvious answer. Then there were those with almost no clues, but the answer was obvious. Sometimes they shifted abruptly into the other category. The longer it dragged on, the more positive Curtis was that this was the first kind.

"So," said Monica, returning and taking a seat beside him. She handed him a plate with a piece of pizza. "Who's Melanie?"

Curtis turned back to her. "Where did you hear about Melanie?"

Monica shrugged. "I was curious, so I googled your wedding last night. Two years, and I've never even heard her name."

"I hadn't heard of Nate either."

"Yeah," said Monica. "I guess we haven't really been speaking."

"We haven't."

"Why?"

"Why what?"

"Why haven't we spoken?"

Curtis shrugged. "I didn't want anything to do with this town after everything that happened."

Monica nodded, although she didn't seem convinced. "You could've stayed. You could have helped us rebuild and make it something to be proud of."

Curtis looked at their father. "That wasn't the life I wanted. I'm so close to getting it. Just before I get everything I've ever wanted, I'm brought back here. I don't believe in

God, but it certainly seems like something He would arrange."

He laughed to himself, almost despite everything.

"What do you mean?"

Curtis looked up at Monica.

"What do you mean 'everything you've ever wanted'?"

Curtis thought of Melanie and was hit with a feeling of guilt. He thought of the promise he had made to come home, and why he had been forced to make it.

"Melanie's pregnant," he said.

Monica stared at him, her mouth slightly agape. "She's pregnant? You're going to be a dad?"

"Yeah."

"When?"

Curtis looked at his sister. She was smiling. It was the smile he remembered from their childhood.

He smiled back at her.

Gordon Mackley mumbled something about being a grandfather. They both jerked their heads toward him.

Gordon Mackley was awake and smiling, watching his two children. His eyes had a clarity that hadn't been there when Curtis had visited him at his house. Gordon was focused on them and clearly understanding what they were saying.

"Dad!" said Monica, leaping up and rushing to his side. "How long have you been awake?"

"A few minutes. I didn't want to disturb your conversation. I'm going to be a grandfather?"

"Yeah," said Curtis, smiling. "She's fifteen weeks along."

Gordon smiled.

Monica stood. "I'll go get the nurse and tell her Dad's awake."

She left and returned a minute later with a nurse at her side.

The nurse checked Gordon's vitals without a huge amount of enthusiasm, made a comment about getting the doctor, and left the room. A few minutes later, the doctor arrived and asked to speak with Monica and Curtis out in the hallway.

"No," said Gordon Mackley. "Anything you tell them, you tell me. Knowing is always better than not knowing, that's my motto. If I'm going to drop dead, tell me to my face."

The doctor turned to Monica and Curtis. Monica shrugged.

"May as well," said Monica. "He can handle it."

"Well," said the doctor. "Vitals are improving, and the stroke won't have any lasting effects on his movement. However, there's an increased risk over the next twenty-four hours or so. If he has another stroke, his chances of survival will be much lower."

They asked the doctor a few questions before thanking him. The doctor retreated from the room.

"Who was that ugly fucker?" said Gordon.

Curtis looked back at him. The fogginess and confusion had returned to Gordon's eyes. He stared at the door without seeming to understand it.

Monica sighed and turned on the television. Gordon absently watched the screen and seemed to get lost in the news program.

"I'm going to grab something to drink," said Monica, putting a hand on Curtis's arm. "Want anything?"

"No, I'm good." Curtis took his seat beside the bed.

Monica left the room, leaving Curtis with the father who had momentarily been the man he remembered.

Curtis looked out the window and over the dark town.

"Thanks for being here, Josh," said Gordon. "I appreciate it."

CHAPTER 30

PATROL CARS HAD BEEN CIRCLING THE TOWN ALL DAY, DIVIDED between protecting the townspeople and searching for Ken Hagerty. Ken's normal hangouts had been investigated and his friends and co-workers interrogated, but nothing had come out of it.

Finally, on the last construction site, Frankie and Trevor found his pickup truck.

They climbed out of the car and walked up to the front door of the immense house.

Frankie held her gun at her side.

Ken's battered truck was parked just inside the fence, shielded from the road.

Frankie climbed up the side of the truck and looked inside. On the back seat, there were a few dark spots that might have been blood.

The truck was high enough that the back seat would be hidden from almost everyone. She dropped onto the ground and nodded to Trevor.

As they walked toward the house, Frankie followed the

footprints which went from the truck to the house. Drops of blood appeared every few feet.

The house had enormous pillars on either side of the door, as though the designer hadn't been able to decide if he was building a house or a castle.

When Frankie tried to open the door, holding her gun in her other hand, she found it was locked. The window three feet away hadn't yet been installed, so they climbed through and landed inside. Trevor took a tumble and made enough noise that anyone inside would have heard.

Frankie looked back at Trevor. He shrugged in apology.

They couldn't hear anything, but there was a light on in the kitchen. They walked toward the light, making sure the rooms on either side of the hall were clear, then entered the kitchen. More light came from the staircase which led into the basement. Frankie motioned for Trevor to follow her and remain quiet.

They walked down the stairs slowly. Frankie winced whenever the stairs creaked.

They rounded the corner into the basement.

Frankie raised her gun as she stepped off the bottom step.

She frowned as she took in the sight at the bottom of the stairs.

"You got me," said Ken Hagerty. He slouched against the far wall, holding a half-finished beer in one hand. He indicated the beer. "It's warm. I should have installed the fridge earlier. I'll make a note of that for future projects."

"Where's Zach?" said Frankie, leveling her gun at him.

Ken pointed behind her. Frankie followed where he was pointing.

"Holy shit," said Trevor, holstering his gun and sprinting over to the hunched-over form in the corner.

Zach wasn't conscious, but there was a steady rise and fall to his stomach which reassured Frankie. His shirt was soaked with blood. There was additional blood leaking from the top of his head. A bloody baseball bat sat a few feet away, cracked in the middle where the wood had splintered. Trevor felt for a pulse while Frankie kept her gun pointed at Ken.

Trevor let out a sigh of relief. "He's alive."

Frankie nodded. "Call an ambulance. I'll deal with Ken."

"Come on," said Ken, holding out his arms. "He's ready to confess. I did that for you."

"He wasn't a suspect."

"Sure he was. The paper said so. "

"The paper was wrong," said Frankie. "Put down the beer and kneel with your hands wrapped behind your head."

"No need to get angry about me doing your job better than you." He knelt and wrapped his fingers together behind his head. "Maybe now you might actually find my fucking daughter."

"Turn around."

"I'm trying to help."

"I will shoot you if you try anything," said Frankie. "You assaulted an innocent boy for no reason. Ashley loved him. What the hell would Ashley think of what you did?"

Ken seemed less sure of himself. "I did it for her."

"Turn the fuck around."

Ken obeyed her and did nothing as she cuffed him. She led him up the stairs just as the paramedics arrived, pointing to the basement where Trevor was waiting with Zach. She walked out of the house to her car, past the flashing lights of the ambulance. She shoved Ken into the back seat and slammed the door in his face. He muttered something as she did so, but she didn't hear him.

The street was mostly vacant. The lights of the ambulance flashed along the houses. Natasha Nolowinski wasn't there, thankfully.

A few minutes later the paramedics exited the house, Zach lying on a stretcher between them. Trevor trailed a few feet behind, watching the high schooler's mutilated body as he clung to life. They loaded Zach into the ambulance and nodded to Frankie.

"We're taking him to Blind River General Hospital," said one of the paramedics as he climbed into the back of the ambulance.

"Will he pull through?" said Frankie.

The other paramedic didn't mince words as he climbed in. "Fifty-fifty."

The doors closed and the ambulance pulled out of the driveway, sirens blaring, and turned down the street toward the hospital.

Trevor stood beside Frankie, watching the lights and the sounds of the sirens recede into the distance. They stood in silence until the ambulance disappeared around a corner.

Ken was shouting something from the back seat about his rights as a father and an American, but neither paid him any attention.

"What now?" said Trevor.

Frankie shrugged. "We bring Ken to the station, interrogate him, and figure out what to do from there. Why does Blind River have a general hospital?"

"The hospital was built along with the prison so that prisoners had somewhere nearby for surgeries. We wouldn't have gotten the prison otherwise."

Frankie nodded. "Let's get Ken back to the station."

They climbed into the car. Ken continued ranting in the back seat.

"If you don't shut up, I will shoot you," said Frankie as she started the car's engine. "I will say it happened when we were rescuing Zach and that it was necessary force. Detective Marshall will back me up, right?"

Trevor hesitated, then nodded.

Ken looked like he was about to say something, but instead sunk into his seat, his cuffed hands held in his lap.

They drove to the police station in silence, the darkness of the town giving cover to who they were transporting.

When they got to the police station, no protesters were waiting for them.

CHAPTER 31

CURTIS SAT BESIDE HIS FATHER'S BED WHILE MONICA SLEPT IN A chair less than a dozen feet away, a half-eaten yogurt beside her. Their father slept, his mumblings still coming through his unfocused haze, the words and sentences unintelligible.

At that moment, Curtis felt closer to his father than he had in a long time.

He'd spoken to Frankie about the arrest of Ken Hagerty and the hospitalization of Zach O'Reilly. Frankie was in the hospital with Zach. Trevor was at the station, trying to figure out what had happened to Zach in that half-finished house.

"Curtis."

Curtis looked up at his father, who was awake and looking at him.

"Where am I?" said Gordon.

"You're in the hospital," said Curtis. "You had a stroke."

Gordon Mackley nodded, as though that only prompted more questions. He looked out the window. "Did you find those girls?"

"What?"

"Those girls who went missing. Did you find them?"

"You know about the girls?"

Gordon smacked his hands down on the bed and shouted, "You know what girls I'm talking about, Curtis. Don't treat me like some kind of mentally handicapped moron. The Hagerty girl and the Matheson girl and the other two."

Curtis looked up at Monica, who had been woken by Gordon's shout. She was watching their father with concern and interest.

"We haven't found them," said Curtis.

Gordon leaned back. Curtis couldn't mistake the clarity in his eyes this time. Gordon was aware of himself, at least for now. "Did you check the forest?" he said. "That's where Marino always buried the bodies."

Curtis nodded. "We checked. K-9 teams were sent through."

"That isn't good enough. You know that as well as I do, Curtis."

"What do you mean?" Curtis looked at Monica, who shrugged.

"Whenever you were out there drinking with your friends," said Gordon. "You hid the beer bottles somewhere."

Curtis laughed at the randomness and absurdity of the memory his father had brought up. It was something Gordon Mackley had accused Curtis of but had never been able to prove: that Curtis and his friends were going to the forest to drink and hide the bottles.

"Come on, Dad," said Curtis. "We never—"

Curtis frowned, staring forward.

Monica leaned forward, watching Curtis.

"Curtis?" said Gordon. "Did you—"

"Everyone shut up!" Curtis stood and focused on a blank spot on the white wall, willing his mind to retrace the path it had been opening up, what he'd been trying to see for days. He stared at the wall, letting his mind trace the path backward, not seeing anything but his own memories. Suddenly, it all came back to him.

"Holy shit," he whispered, his eyes widening.

"What?" said Monica. She and Gordon wore the same confused expression.

"I need your car keys," said Curtis. "It might be nothing. Stay with Dad." Curtis grabbed his coat from the back of the chair.

"Where are you going?" said Monica, handing him the keys.

He snatched the keys from her hand. "To check something. Stay with Dad."

Before Monica could say another word, Curtis was out the door, marching down the hallway. The nurses stepped out of his way as they saw him approaching. Curtis left the hospital and climbed into Monica's detective car.

It was only halfway through his drive that he wondered if the person he needed to meet had moved.

As soon as he pulled up to the house, he knew it was the right place. He would have recognized the SUV in the driveway anywhere. There was also a red car in the driveway which he recognized, but couldn't place.

He shrugged it off, assuming it must be a car he had seen around town and walked to the front door. Although it was getting late, the lights were still on inside. The sounds of television and laughter came through the window. Curtis knocked on the door and stepped back. He put his hands in his pockets.

There was some confused conversation from inside, and the door opened.

Jeff Parker stood in the doorway, still dressed in the jeans he would have worn working as a math teacher at the school earlier that day. Curtis remembered the day he'd found out Jeff had been working for Marino, the day their friendship had begun disintegrating.

"Curtis?" said Jeff, frowning. "It's late. What are you doing here?"

"I need to speak with you."

"Why's that?"

"Who is it?" said another voice. A woman ran up to the front door. "Oh, hi, Agent Mackley."

Curtis frowned, looking at Kelly Oberman and Jeff Parker close to one another, wondering how it had never occurred to him they would know each other. Kelly Oberman still had red eyes from crying, and she stood close to Jeff.

"Miss Oberman," said Curtis. "How are you?"

"I'm fine. Do you have any leads on Darcy?"

"I need to talk to Jeff. It might be difficult to hear."

"Come on," said Kelly, taking Jeff with her out onto the front step with her and closing the door. "What is it?"

Kelly crossed her arms. Curtis was once again baffled at how young she was, that she could have two children, one a cop and the other in high school.

Jeff crossed his arms as well and waited for Curtis to speak.

"When we were kids," said Curtis, "Do you remember we used to drink in the woods?"

Jeff shrugged. "Sure. We'd got some beer and head out there. That was after Marino was imprisoned, but before you ditched Blind River. It was also before you found out I'd been working for him. What's your point?"

"Remember we would ditch the beer bottles in the river, and they would never show up again?"

Jeff frowned, as though he could feel where Curtis was going, then his eyes opened wide. "Holy shit. Are you thinking what I'm thinking?"

Curtis shrugged. "It's worth checking out."

Jeff nodded, any animosity evaporating. "I know where it is. We can take your car. Kelly, stay here."

"What?" said Kelly. "I'm coming with you."

"Stay here. This is between me and Curtis."

"What?"

Curtis and Jeff had already climbed into the detective car and pulled out of the driveway. Kelly shouted after them that it was about her daughter.

They drove out onto the road, with Jeff directing.

"So," said Curtis, trying to get some sort of conversation going, "how long have you and Kelly Oberman been a thing?"

"On and off for a few years now. Nothing serious. Turn left here."

Curtis nodded. "What are your thoughts on Bobby Randall?"

"Bobby Randall? Robert Randall's kid? Seems like a bit of a deadbeat to me. Never amounted to anything. Why are you asking about him?"

"Because he told me Marino wanted my head."

Jeff was silent for a long moment, then said, "Bobby would know that."

"Why?"

"Because he was in prison with Marino."

"I've spoken to Marino."

"And?" Jeff seemed like he was trying too hard to appear uninterested.

"Nothing, except he claimed to know who was kidnapping the girls."

"Don't listen to him, Curtis. You know better than that."

"I know, but if he does know, then we need his cooperation."

"Do not listen to him," Jeff said it with such anger that he seemed genuine. Maybe something had changed in the time Curtis had been gone. "Marino will tear you apart."

Curtis looked out at the forest in front of them. "I recognize this place. It's here."

"Park here."

Curtis parked on the side of the road. The forest stretched out before them, enveloping the darkness. He exited the car and took out a flashlight. He shined it between the seemingly endless trees. The police had already sent a team of dogs through here, but if Curtis's hunch was right, they hadn't checked everywhere.

They couldn't have. Curtis and Jeff hadn't told anyone.

"Are you sure this is the right place?" said Curtis, shining the flashlight back and forth.

"This is the right place," said Jeff, standing beside him. "It's grown over a bit. Let's go."

Jeff hesitated before walking into the trees.

Curtis knew how he felt. If they were right, they would wish they weren't.

As they walked, their feet trampled over fallen leaves and

branches only recently released from the snow. The leaves crunched beneath their feet. Jeff navigated while Curtis held the flashlight.

Jeff got lost only once and recovered quickly.

Curtis checked his watch. It was nearly midnight. The adrenaline was keeping him going, but his limited sleep over the last couple days was beginning to catch up with him.

If not for Jeff putting a hand in front of his chest, Curtis would have walked right into the Blind River.

It wasn't so much a river as it was a pond created by a widening of the river which flowed into the center of town.

"This is it," said Curtis, aiming his flashlight down at the pond. It had served them well during their high school years.

"The Blind River," said Jeff, smirking at the inside joke only he and Curtis knew, although he looked like he was about to hurl. "How can we check?"

Curtis shined the flashlight into the murky depths of the water. The flashlight beam didn't make it more than three feet beneath the surface. He and Jeff had discovered this pond while they were in high school.

In a moment of panic, as a teacher found them in the woods, they'd thrown a six pack of Budweiser into the nearest pond. Once they were certain they'd gotten away with it, they went back to retrieve the beer.

They couldn't see the beer in the pond, as though it had vanished into thin air.

Initially, they'd thought someone else had found it, but, on a hunch of Jeff's, they'd tried again. When the bottles hit the bottom of the pond, the mud wrapped around them like comforting arms until it was like they'd never existed. The bottom of the pond was a sinkhole from which nothing returned. They'd never understood it but had used it as much as possible. They had often joked that this was where Blind River had truly gotten its name.

Now, Curtis was hoping he was wrong about something else hidden in the mud.

"Hold this." He handed Jeff the flashlight and took off his jacket.

"Are you serious?" said Jeff, raising an eyebrow. "You're crazy."

"I have to. It's the only way to know." Curtis undressed, leaving just his underwear and t-shirt.

He then took off the t-shirt, feeling the chill of nighttime air on his nude chest.

He stepped into the pond all at once, not giving himself time to reconsider. He cursed as the cold water engulfed his body. Although the pond wasn't wide, it was deep, and he had to tread water to keep above the surface.

"Anything?" said Jeff, standing a few feet away.

"Not yet," said Curtis. "Shine the flashlight into the water so I can see. I'm going to dive down."

Jeff nodded. His right leg was shaking. He raised the flashlight above his head and illuminated the water.

Curtis took a deep breath and dove into its depths. The cold water enveloped him, his lungs instantly crying out at him to surface.

He found the bottom of the pond and began sliding his hands through the mud, trying to find something that would indicate he was right.

His hand brushed against the mud of the bottom of the pond. He knew there were countless things here that could cut him, but he had to keep looking.

He began digging through the mud, his lungs screaming at him to surface. He couldn't give up. Somehow he was certain he was right. He moved the mud away.

His heart leaped when his hand brushed something different, something smooth yet wrinkled at the same time.

He jerked his hand away and immediately felt blood seeping from his hand, warmer than the rest of his body. He had cut it on something.

His hand screamed in pain, mixed with the screaming of his lungs. Through his eyelids, Curtis could feel the flashlight beam moving back and forth across the top of the water.

Jeff was probably standing on the edge of the pond, panicking, wondering if an FBI agent had died on his watch. Curtis's blood would be reaching the surface, making a circle of red in the middle of the beam.

Curtis couldn't focus on that now. He had to know. He moved his uninjured hand back, looking for what he'd touched before.

He needed to be sure.

At the moment before his instincts took over and forced him to surface, he found what he'd touched before.

He grabbed it.

His heart sank.

He was right.

With a heavy heart, he released the small feminine hand sticking up from the mud at the bottom of the pond and let himself float to the surface.

CHAPTER 32

THE FIRST BODY WAS PULLED FROM THE WATER AT FOUR o'clock on Saturday morning. A call to the FBI had scrambled a dive and retrieval team who had arrived three hours after Curtis had grabbed the hand at the bottom of the pond.

The FBI team carried the desecrated body out of the water and laid it out on the large tarp. It was illuminated by spotlights, which the FBI team had set up around the pond.

The body was unrecognizable, the skin rotting and peeling away. Only the hand Curtis had grabbed still looked alive. The clothes the girl had worn hung off her like rags. Her hair could have been brunette, blonde or red for all Curtis could see.

Curtis sat on a folding chair fifty feet away from the pond. He had a blanket wrapped around him and a cup of hot chocolate between his hands. His right hand was wrapped in thick, blood-stained bandages.

Jeff was standing nearby, explaining the situation to Frankie. Trevor moved around the site, coordinating with police and newly arrived FBI agents. Monica was still at the hospital with their father.

A pile of beer bottles retrieved by the FBI team sat beside the pond. Curtis wondered how many were his and Jeff's, and who else had known about this place.

The searchers were shouting that they had a second body. Moments later, the second body was pulled out. It was in a worse state than the first, with no defining features remaining.

Frankie sighed and walked up to Curtis, leaving Jeff behind. "We'll fingerprint the first one," she said. "There won't be fingerprints for the others. Identifying them is going to be a challenge."

"No kidding."

Jeff walked up to them. He put a hand on Curtis's shoulder. "Kelly's coming."

"This isn't supposed to be public yet," said Curtis. "What about the other parents?"

"They're coming, too."

"Jesus Christ." Curtis shook off the blanket, stood, and began pacing. "They can't be allowed to see their daughters yet."

"They deserve to have closure."

"And we don't have it yet. We have two bodies."

"Three." Jeff pointed to a third body being hauled from the pond and placed on the tarp. It looked barely human.

"How did Kelly find out?"

"I think Officer Oberman told her," said Jeff. "Officer Hagerty might have done the same with his sister-in-law."

"Damn." Curtis rubbed his eyes. "Can you console Kelly? If anyone asks, the bodies will be available for viewing and identification at the medical examiner's office first thing in the morning. Seven o'clock. Any questions?"

"I got it." Jeff went to leave and then turned back. "Curtis?"

"Yeah?"

"Thanks for trusting me. After all, that happened between us, with Marino."

Curtis shrugged. "You would have done the same for me."

"No, I wouldn't have," said Jeff.

"Don't say that."

"It was me, Curtis."

Curtis turned towards him. "What?"

Jeff took a deep breath. "I'm the one who told Marino you ratted him out."

Curtis nodded, as though it made perfect sense, although his mind was reeling. "Marino knows what I did? Without any doubt in your mind?"

"He knows everything. I told him. I'm sorry." Jeff turned to leave.

There was a screech of tires. Screaming erupted from the perimeter of the forest a few hundred yards away. Curtis had always found it morbidly interesting how distinct the cry of a mother was. No matter what the context, there was something about the desperation and fear that distinguished it from any other scream.

"I have to go," said Jeff, sprinting toward the screaming.

Frankie approached Curtis, and he explained what had happened. She looked past him and sighed.

"And there's the fourth body," she said.

CHAPTER 33

CURTIS AND FRANKIE TRIED AND FAILED TO SLEEP AT THE police station.

Curtis spent most of the time thinking about Marino. At least Jeff seemed to be on his side.

At half past six, they were handed cups of mild coffee.

Frankie and Trevor had spent a few hours the previous night interviewing Ken Hagerty, but they had failed to get anything important.

Ken had continued to claim everything he'd done was in the best interests of his daughter. His victim, Zach O'Reilly, had been put into a medically-induced coma while the doctors tried desperately to save his life. The charges against Ken depended on whether or not Zach pulled through.

Trevor had gone home, citing a need for sleep, and Monica had called in from the hospital to get the details. There had been no change in Gordon Mackley's status.

The FBI divers had declared there was nothing else to be found in the pond and boarded the plane back Manhattan.

The Blind River was still taped off and guarded by police officers.

Once the town began to wake up, there would be a frenzy to see the site and hear what had happened to the victims.

Curtis and Frankie were led to the Medical Examiner's Office, where the bodies would be identified by family members. Curtis had dealt with these situations before, and he knew that the family members would be experiencing a strange mix of anguish that their loved ones were dead and relief that they finally had answers, even if they weren't what they wanted.

The bodies were laid out on four tables side by side, sheets covering them from head to toe. The medical examiner was a red-haired woman who introduced herself as Dr. Marie Novak.

"So," said Frankie, standing beside Dr. Novak. "What's the report?"

"Not good," said Dr. Novak. "I was unable to identify three of them. The only successful identification was Darcy Oberman. She's the third body from the left. It was because of her height. The others are harder. I took prints from the first one pulled out of the water, but she isn't in the system. Harriet Matheson is the only one of the four victims who has prints in the FBI database, so that only crosses her out as being the first body. I sent out DNA samples, but who knows how long that'll take. I'll try to get some from the parents and see if I can get a match."

Frankie nodded and turned to one of the officers with them. "Are the parents here yet? They can identify them."

Dr. Novak frowned and glanced at the desecrated bodies.

"They can't—" She stopped talking when Frankie glared at her. "Of course."

Frankie turned and leaned out of the room. Curtis couldn't hear what she was saying to someone outside.

A few minutes later, an officer walked into the room with Kelly Oberman and Jeff Parker.

Matt Oberman followed a few steps behind, looking far more nervous than his mother about seeing and identifying his sister's body. Jeff had his arm draped around Kelly, who was holding her hands just below her eyes, ready to hide from the world at a moment's notice. Her eyes were red, as though she'd run out of tears to cry.

"Ms. Oberman," said Dr. Novak, pulling Kelly into a hug. "Thank you for coming in. I understand how hard this must be."

Kelly nodded.

"Where is she?" said Jeff, making eye contact with Curtis.

"Come with me," said Dr. Novak, walking around the table to the body marked number three. She put her hands on either side of the sheet. "You need to be aware of what the body has been through. I've found no signs she died in any pain or suffering. The vast majority of what you're about to see happened after death. Are you ready?"

All eyes turned to Kelly, who stared at the sheet, below which her daughter's body lay. She nodded almost imperceptibly. Dr. Novak reached under the back of the sheet and lifted it over the girl's head.

Kelly let out a long and loud cry, mimicking the one she'd given at the edge of the forest a few hours earlier. From deep within her, she seemed to find more tears to cry. Jeff pulled her close, shielding her from the image of her daughter's decaying face, the skin missing from Darcy's right cheek. Curtis and Frankie stood back, letting the events unfold before them.

"I'm sorry for your loss," said Dr. Novak, reaching out a hand and putting it on Kelly's shoulder.

"It's her," said Kelly without removing her face from Jeff's shoulder. "It's her. It's Darcy. It's my daughter."

"Thank you," said Dr. Novak. "If there's anything that I can help with—"

"No," said Kelly. She looked up at Jeff. "Let's go."

Jeff hesitated for a moment, looking around to see if there was anything else to do. When Curtis shook his head, he moved out of the room with Kelly.

Officer Oberman stayed a few seconds longer, staring at his sister's dead face, his expression blank, completely devoid of any emotion at all, then followed his mother and Jeff out of the room.

Curtis rubbed his eyes and indicated to the officer by the door to bring in the next family. If he had to choose one part of the job he could go without, it would be this. He could handle dead bodies. There was nothing left for them. The person they had once been was gone. The families, though, had to live with the misery, pain, and absence of their loved ones.

The doors to the Medical Examiner's Office opened and Kendra, and Oscar Matheson entered. Oscar looked relatively sober, although whether that was because he wanted to look respectable or because it was too early in the morning to be drunk, Curtis couldn't tell.

Oscar trailed a few feet behind his eldest daughter. They both came to a stop at the bottom of the tables where the bodies were laid out.

"Where's my daughter?" said Oscar, monotone.

Dr. Novak stepped forward. "That's why we invited you here. It's very important that you remain calm and understand this is a very delicate situation."

"What are you talking about?" said Oscar. "Just show me my daughter's body and get it over with."

Kendra glanced at her father.

"That's the issue," said Dr. Novak, looking uncomfortable. Curtis guessed this was a first for her as well. "We don't know which body is Harriet's."

"What?" said Kendra.

"We've only identified one body. Number three is Darcy Oberman. The other three are beyond recognition."

"What?" said Oscar, looking as though he wanted to vomit. "Are you serious? You mean she might not be here? She might still be out there with some madman?"

"Mr. Matheson," said Dr. Novak, "we're very confident we have the bodies of four kidnapped girls. We'll be taking DNA samples from you and the other families to guarantee it."

Oscar seemed unable to speak, so Kendra said, "What do you need us to do?"

"If you feel up to it," said Dr. Novak, "We want you to look at the three unidentified bodies, and tell us which one you think is Harriet."

Oscar put his hand over his mouth and clenched his eyes shut.

"We'll do what we can," said Kendra, swallowing but mostly hiding her fear.

Slowly, Dr. Novak removed the sheets from the heads of

the three unidentified bodies and showed them to the Mathesons.

Dr. Novak handed Oscar a barf bag from beside the sink. He dry-heaved into the bag for a few moments, then looked up and nodded, his face white. He kept the bag at chest level.

Kendra moved around the table, looking at the desecrated faces of the three girls. "This one," she said, pointing to the body on the far left.

"Are you sure?" said Dr. Novak. "How can you tell?"

"I just know." Kendra went to touch the rotting nose, then pulled her hand back. "It's her."

All eyes turned to Oscar, still holding the barf bag close, who nodded. "It's her. I'd recognize my little girl anywhere."

"Thank you," said Curtis, stepping forward and putting a hand on Oscar's shoulder. "I'm sure you'll want to make arrangements. Harriet's body will be released as soon as Dr. Novak is done and we've learned everything we can to find her killer."

"Thank you," said Oscar, wringing his hands as he was led out of the room by his only remaining daughter. Curtis wondered how long it would be until Oscar was wasted.

He thought of Melanie and the child that would be arriving in less than five months.

The third family was the Hagertys. Joe Hagerty walked in with his sister-in-law, Miriam. She looked braver than Curtis would've guessed.

Ken Hagerty wasn't permitted to leave his cell. Curtis was sure he was angry about it.

Miriam requested it be over with quickly. She identified Ashley based on a scar below her ear almost immediately. She thanked everyone there and was escorted out without showing any emotion at all. Somehow, that was more unsettling to Curtis than the crying of the others.

As Miriam Hagerty was led from the room, Curtis prepared himself for the last of the parents, the O'Connells, to come in and identify their daughter.

"Excuse me, Agent Mackley," said one of the officers in the room.

Curtis turned to face him. "Yes?"

"Ken Hagerty is putting up quite a ruckus," said the officer. "He says he'll do anything to see his daughter before she gets buried."

Curtis sighed. He understood the man's desperation. He'd seen it many times. He also didn't think there was any chance Ken would confess. Regardless, he needed to check.

"You good here?" he said to Frankie.

"I'll be fine," said Frankie.

Curtis nodded and followed the officer into the main bullpen, walking past where Reba and Gareth O'Connell were waiting, holding each other's hands and dressed in their Sunday best.

They met Curtis's eyes as he walked past, but didn't acknowledge him. In that glance, Curtis felt like they were blaming him, as though finding the body of their daughter had actually been the thing that killed her. Maybe, they were thinking, that if Curtis had stayed out of it, they could still believe their daughter was alive and happy somewhere.

Curtis turned the corner and walked toward the cells. The officer opened the door to the cell block. Curtis stepped inside. The door closed behind him and locked.

Ken Hagerty, leaning through the bars, looked up at him.

"Agent Mackley," he said, "let me see my daughter. It's my

right as a father. I've got to see her." His voice rose as he continued, but there was a sense of defeat underlying his words. "You're trampling on my rights as an American. I have a right to see my daughter before they put her into the ground."

Curtis stood a few feet from the bars, looking in at Ken Hagerty like he was a wild animal. "Sign a confession," he said. "I'll get a judge to let you out to see the funeral."

"I did what any father would do," said Ken. "I'm not signing shit."

"Then there's nothing I can do." Curtis turned on his heel and began to walk away.

"Come on, man," said Ken, shifting from anger to desperation, pleading. "She's my only daughter. She was my everything. I've got nothing left. Just try to understand."

Curtis turned and walked back to Ken. He took his phone out of his pocket and scrolled to a photo of Zach O'Reilly in the hospital. Zach's face was a red and black mess of bruises. Half his body was in a variety of casts. Tubes and wires connected him to machines keeping him alive.

"See this?" said Curtis, holding up the picture to Ken, who turned away just a little. "You did this. How do you think his parents feel? He and Ashley loved each other. For that, you put him in the hospital, and you might have killed him. How would you feel if it was Zach who was missing and Mr. O'Reilly had kidnapped and beaten Ashley half to death?"

Ken looked like he would cave for just a moment. Instead, he said, "That doesn't matter. It was my Ashley who was missing. Screw them to hell. They don't understand. I would beat the shit out of a million Zach O'Reilly's if it got my daughter back."

Curtis sighed and put his phone back into his pocket. "When you're ready to confess and apologize to that family for what you've done, let me know, and we'll talk. Until then, enjoy the cell."

Curtis turned and walked out of the jail, ignoring the screams and curses hurled after him. He breathed a sigh of relief when the door to the jail closed behind him.

The silence only lasted a moment before he heard a wail coming from the Medical Examiner's Office on the other side of the station.

He turned the corner and saw the O'Connells being led out of the station by a few officers. He couldn't tell whether the wail had come from the wife or the husband. They were both hunched over and incapable of answering any questions from the officers. They left the station without looking back.

"You get anything?" said Frankie, walking up and standing beside Curtis.

"Nothing," said Curtis. "You?"

"It took longer than the others, but they identified Miranda. Dr. Novak is going to start examining them to figure out the exact causes of death."

Curtis raised an eyebrow. "It wasn't drowning?"

Frankie shook her head. "No. Strangulation seems to be the leading candidate. There are indications that their windpipes were crushed. Novak says it seems like it's the only thing the killer did. No rape, no assault, just knocked them out and crushed their windpipes."

Curtis nodded. "I need to speak to Marino again. Jeff was the one who told Marino about my involvement in his arrest."

Frankie said, "You need a ride?"

"Drop me off at the hospital. Monica is there with our dad. He's not doing well. I'll borrow Monica's car."

"Okay."

Curtis glanced at Frankie. He had noticed that Frankie's ferocity always began to wear off as a case wore on. They had never been on a case long enough for her to lose her focus and become incapable, but Curtis wondered if they would ever need to confront that possibility.

"I have something I need to investigate," said Frankie.

"What?"

"We're getting close to finding the killer. I need to silence Natasha. I'm going to try to dig something up on her to stop her from writing articles until the case is over."

"You don't think we should focus on finding the leak?"

Frankie shook her head. "It'll take too long to find the leak. We can guarantee her silence this way. I'll get a warrant to search her computer and her home. Come on, let's go."

They left the station.

Curtis felt uneasy about arresting Natasha for something unrelated to their case, but he knew Frankie well enough to know she saw no issue. Frankie saw no problem with using any tool at her disposal to solve the cases she was assigned to. Curtis disagreed.

That balance had always been both the reason they worked well as partners and the basis of most of their arguments.

They drove to the hospital. Curtis thanked Frankie as he climbed out.

He walked into the hospital and took the elevator to the fourth floor. He knocked on the door of his father's room, and

Monica opened the door, putting a finger to her lips. They walked inside in silence.

"He's sleeping," said Monica softly. "I heard you found the bodies."

"Yeah." Curtis walked to the side of the bed. Gordon Mackley slept soundly, his head lolled to one side. The rhythmic beeping of the machines was a reassuring reminder that his father was still alive. "What did the doctors say?"

Monica shrugged. "If he makes it to tonight, his odds are fifty-fifty. If he makes it through the next week, then it goes to ninety-ten."

"So today matters."

"I guess so."

"Anything I can do?"

"There's nothing more even the doctors can do. Just wait."

"Okay." He took a seat beside his father, putting a hand on his sleeping shoulder. "Get better, Dad."

He stayed there, watching his father sleep, for what seemed like too long and too short at the same time.

He asked Monica for her car keys, explaining that he needed to speak with Marino. She nodded and handed him the keys without any questions. He walked to the door.

"Curtis?" said Monica.

He turned back.

Monica was staring out the window. "If you can, find out what happened to Josh. It would mean a lot to Dad."

Curtis nodded, then closed the door slowly so as not to wake his father.

CHAPTER 34

FRANKIE ARRIVED AT THE CHURCH AND WALKED THROUGH THE front doors. She'd called Chief Tucker and explained what she needed to do. The chief had agreed on the condition that Trevor come with her. She couldn't be acting independently in a situation this delicate. Tucker was worried that the town was slipping back into its old ways, and Frankie couldn't blame him.

The church was a basic Presbyterian chapel. She looked through the stained-glass windows at the front of the chapel depicting the crucifixion of Christ. She gave the Son of God a curt nod and closed her eyes for a moment, asking for help.

She opened her eyes with new confidence. She took a deep breath and touched the cross necklace beneath her shirt.

She reached into her pocket for her notepad, taking the opportunity to look through her notes. She took out the notepad she'd taken from Natasha's desk, then continued going through her pocket.

Her eyes went wide.

It wasn't there.

The last time she'd had it was at the last of the family interviews. Since then she hadn't needed to take notes, and the familiar weight of a notepad, Natasha's notepad, in her pocket had blocked any subconscious suspicions.

"Shit," she muttered under her breath. A minister sitting on one of the pews looked up at her and closed the Bible he was reading. He stood and walked toward her.

Frankie suddenly smiled. She remembered Natasha reaching for her jacket when she'd been at the offices of the Blind River Observer. Stealing a notepad from a federal agent was a crime worthy of being incarcerated until well after the conclusion of the case.

Frankie wouldn't even need to make anything up.

The minister walked up to Frankie. He had grey hair and glasses. He looked experienced and calm.

"Is there anything I can help you with?" he said.

"I'm looking for the Alcoholics Anonymous meeting," she told him, "specifically for Trevor Marshall."

The minister nodded. "Downstairs. I spoke with Trevor less than half an hour ago. This entire case has been difficult on him." The minister looked her up and down. "You're the FBI agent. Curtis Mackley's partner."

Frankie nodded. She didn't want to disrupt the AA meeting. She understood their sanctity. She'd walked in on one of her father's meetings once. He'd been angry for months.

She held out a hand. "Special Agent Frankie Lassiter. You knew Curtis?"

The minister nodded and shook her hand. "The town knows me as Father Bryan. I knew the entire Mackley clan. They're good people with a bewildering streak of naivety. It was always a trait in the family. I suppose you're looking for those girls."

"Yes."

"I've been praying for them. Hopefully, God will provide, and they'll be returned home safely."

Frankie nodded, realizing that Father Bryan didn't know. She stared forward, through the pews which lined the sides of the chapel.

Father Bryan turned to her, frowning. "Has something happened?"

"They won't be coming home," she said softly.

Father Bryan turned away. "They're somewhere better now," he said. "They can rest in peace."

The minister let out a sigh that could only have come from a man who'd seen too much, who had resolved to simply take each day as it came with a smile and a willingness to help people.

It occurred to Frankie that he would have been the town's minister for the duration of the Sam Marino era.

Father Bryan checked his watch. "The meeting will be getting out soon. I'll leave you to speak with Trevor. If you are looking for guidance, Agent Lassiter, you should come to service tomorrow morning."

Frankie sighed. "I don't have time."

Father Bryan turned to leave. "Think about it. I'm sure the locals would appreciate it."

Frankie nodded. "I'll think about it."

"I'll pray for you and Curtis."

"Thank you."

Father Bryan retreated toward the office door at the side of the chapel lobby. Frankie was left standing alone for a few moments before the door to the basement opened, and sounds of conversation flooded out.

A stream of people walked past her, shooting her nervous glances. Trevor was one of the last people out of the basement.

He paused when he saw Frankie. He walked up to her after saying goodbye to the people around him.

"What are you doing here?" he said.

"We have a job to do," she said.

"What job?"

"Natasha Nolowinski."

Trevor sighed. "What did she do now?"

"She stole my notepad."

Trevor turned and looked at her. "She did?"

"Yes. I was going to make something up to get her out of the way, but now I don't need to."

"If we arrest her, there will be a backlash," said Trevor. "We can't have this city turn against us. Too many people listen to her."

"It's worth it."

Trevor nodded and smiled. "I couldn't have said it better. Let's go get that bitch."

CHAPTER 35

CURTIS WAS MET BY NATE WILLIAMS JUST INSIDE THE entrance of the prison.

They didn't say a word to one another as they walked.

Curtis was led into an interview room.

Harry Ochre led Marino in from the other side of the room. The guards left the two of them alone once Marino was cuffed to the table.

Marino had a somber look. "I heard you found the girls," he said. "I'm sorry. I thought maybe they would still be alive, but I wouldn't have bet on it. Not with who you're looking for."

"Let's cut the shit, Sam," said Curtis, leaning in. "I'm the one who put you here. We both know that. You have two options. You can either tell me what you know about the killer, and we can reduce your sentence by five years, or you can admit that you don't know shit."

"You know," said Marino, leaning forward so his cuffed hands could pick something out of his teeth, "when Jeff told me it was you, I was furious. I told anyone who would listen that I was going to put a shotgun to your balls and fire up, leaving you to bleed out on the side of the road somewhere. But you know what I realized? I realized it was my own fault more than anything. I never suspected that the little twerp who delivered our papers would rat on me, even though he was the chief's son. I should've known, though. Everyone else in my entire organization was under a heavy vetting process, and I got cocky. You beat me. I'm impressed by that. You deserve whatever role the FBI gave you."

"That isn't an answer," said Curtis. "What are you going to tell me?"

Marino looked up at him and smiled. "What would you be willing to give me for information about Josh?"

Images of his brother flashed through Curtis's mind, but he needed to find the killer first.

"Nothing right now," said Curtis. "This is about those girls."

Marino leaned back and smiled. "Then you've got me at a disadvantage, Curtis. I don't know anything."

"What are you talking about? Every time I've been here you've insisted you know exactly who the killer is."

Marino shrugged. "It was fun while it lasted, Curtis. When I get out of here, maybe I'll let you join Josh." He stood, the chain holding his hands to the table pulled tight. "Guards! I'd like to return to my cell now."

"Wait," said Curtis. "What did you say about Josh?"

"Did I say that? I didn't mean to." Marino grinned, staring at him. Harry appeared at the door, waiting for Curtis to indicate he could take the prisoner.

"Take him," said Curtis with a heavy heart. "He doesn't know anything."

Marino said, "I look forward to our next talk."

Curtis was left alone in the room.

He looked at his reflection in the one-way mirror, not knowing whether someone was watching and not caring. What he cared about was the desperate look in his own eyes, his disheveled hair, his messy clothing. He saw someone who had let himself go and had let a case get to him. He let out a deep sigh and decided to see this through to the end. That was all he needed to do.

He stood and walked out of the room.

Nate Williams was standing outside the room, looking at Curtis, concerned. Curtis ignored him and walked out of the prison with Nate a few steps behind. Curtis would never get used to the reverence with which FBI agents were treated.

He drove away from the prison with the radio on full blast and the air conditioning on high, letting him think about nothing for just a few minutes while he drove back to Blind River.

CHAPTER 36

WITH A TEAM OF POLICE OFFICERS BEHIND THEM, FRANKIE AND
Trevor marched into the offices of the Blind River Observer,
despite the secretary's protests.

Frankie held up the warrant, which caused the secretary
to grow quiet.

Frankie, Trevor and the officers marched through the
crowd of confused reporters, who were hurriedly trying to
put out a second edition of that day's paper to announce the
discovery of the bodies.

Natasha didn't notice them until Frankie was leaning over
the edge of her cubicle.

"Hey Natasha," she said when Natasha looked up.

Trevor blocked Natasha's exit from the cubicle.

"Agent Lassiter?" said Natasha. "To what do I owe the
pleasure?"

Frankie reached over the cubicle and flicked the heads of
one of the Red Sox bobbleheads on the desk.

"Natasha," she said, "I was just speaking with my good
friend Trevor Marshall, and I went to show him my notes."

Natasha raised an eyebrow. "What did he say?"

"Well, nothing," said Frankie. "It was strange because I couldn't find my notepad."

Natasha shrugged. "I don't have it."

"Do you mind if I check your desk?"

Natasha stood and got in Frankie's face. "Yes, I do mind. It's private property."

Frankie held up the warrant.

Natasha smirked. "This won't work. I don't have it."

"You're under arrest," said Frankie. "We have warrants to search your home and office for my notepad, which is federal property."

Natasha stood as two officers came into the cubicle behind her. "You won't find your notepad," she said.

Somehow, Frankie knew that was true. They wouldn't find the notepad. Natasha would have disposed of it. However, they had enough evidence to hold her for the time being.

The officers took out a pair of handcuffs, but Natasha shook her head. "Don't use those. I'll come with you, but you'll regret this. Just think of the story I'm going to write about this. Before it was small-time, but corruption and lying within the FBI is a story worthy of a Pulitzer."

Frankie looked around the office at the other reporters, none of whom seemed surprised nor even cared that Natasha was being arrested. Some of them had already gone back to work.

Frankie turned back to Natasha. "You think you're some big shot reporter, don't you? You think you're better than this rag you write for, but can't fathom why you can't get another job. You want to know what I think? I think you're a pathetic and talentless—"

Natasha spat in her face, the spit landing on Frankie's right cheek.

Frankie took a deep breath, restraining herself. She grabbed a Kleenex from the box on Natasha's desk and wiped off her face.

"Why did you do that?" said Frankie.

"You act like you're so much better than me," said Natasha. "This entire thing is bullshit, and you know it." She smiled and leaned in, whispering so only Frankie could hear her. "You won't catch the killer," she said. "He's smarter than you. A lot smarter."

Frankie remembered what Kendra Matheson had told her about Natasha knowing something.

"What do you know, Natasha?" she said calmly. "Tell me what you know, and who's telling you, and we can make this all go away."

Natasha shook her head and smirked. "You missed your chance to ask for my help, Agent."

Frankie turned to Trevor. "Take her away. She's full of it."

Natasha just grinned, as though she was barely holding herself back from breaking out laughing as she was led out of the Blind River Observer to the waiting police car. Frankie watched the car pull out and drive away, wondering how many people in this town knew something about the case she didn't.

CHAPTER 37

FRANKIE MET CURTIS OUTSIDE THE POLICE STATION. THE oppressive sun beat down on them.

"You got Nolowinski?" said Curtis.

"She's waiting in one of the jail cells," said Frankie. "I told her I'd be there soon, make her worried for a bit. She's sitting across from Ken Hagerty. Can't imagine he has anything nice to say to her."

"Good. I don't think Marino knows anything, and even if he does, he isn't interested in talking."

Frankie nodded. "Natasha played the same card. She claimed to know who the killer is."

"We can hold her on that. Not to mention the spitting."

"I know. I'm going to interrogate her after she stews for a bit. Teams of officers are searching for my notepad now, but I don't think they'll find it."

Curtis sighed. "We can get back to focusing on the missing girls."

Neither said what they were both thinking. Without a

break in the case soon, they might never find the killer. He could already be a thousand miles away.

They walked inside the police station and into the war room. Trevor was already inside. Chief Tucker sat to his right. A few minutes later Monica entered, explaining that she had left the nurses in charge of Gordon Mackley for the sake of staying involved in the case. Curtis wanted to tell her to go back, but he knew he'd do exactly the same.

"Okay," said Frankie, walking over to the board where there were already dozens of photos and notes connected by strings. "We've cleared out all external concerns, and now we can focus entirely on the investigation. You have all those files I asked for?"

"Right here," said Chief Tucker, patting the boxes piled on the table. "All the records of known criminals, anyone with a criminal record who was in town on the days of the disappearances, and all case files within a hundred-mile radius which match the M.O. We've gone through everything, including every potential connection to Sam Marino's organization, and we've got nothing. We have Natasha and Ken Hagerty in the cells. We can interrogate them."

"Natasha won't talk right now," said Frankie. "Give her some time to stew. Ken doesn't know anything. We'll see how Natasha's fanbase responds to her imprisonment and go from there. Everyone grab a box and start going through the files. Anything we missed, any connection between the cases whatsoever, we need to find."

They each took a seat around the table and began going through the boxes at a frantic pace. With five of them, the chief included, locked away in the war room, they moved through the boxes at a high speed. The sheer quantity of files still took them almost eight hours to complete, by which time the station was mostly empty.

They took a fifteen-minute break, mandated by Frankie. They then divided up the files which had been listed as likely to be related and started again. The sun outside the windows descended.

Curtis leaned back in his chair, staring at the wall in front of him where everything was pinned and connected. He stared at the wall, urging the mess of strings and pictures to configure themselves into something resembling order. He rubbed his eyes and sipped at his coffee. He stood and looked at the other four, all of whom were in similar states of concentration, all staring at the wall in front of them.

Curtis glanced at his almost empty cup. "Anyone want more coffee?"

Trevor and Monica nodded. Chief Tucker shook his head.

"Frankie?" said Curtis. "You want anything?"

Frankie didn't respond. She was transfixed, staring at the wall with a focused expression.

"Frankie?"

"Be quiet," she said softly.

Curtis opened his mouth to speak, then thought better of it. Frankie stared at the wall as the other four stared at her. The silence stretched on until Curtis was about to say something. Frankie jumped to a standing position and walked to the wall with a triumphant smile.

"Miranda O'Connell," she said. "That's the key."

Curtis frowned. "What do you mean?"

Frankie walked to the center of the wall, where the pictures of the four girls were pinned, and began going down the lists of information.

Frankie grabbed the picture of Miranda O'Connell. "She's the odd one out. She's the only person who left evidence, and the only person kidnapped from a residential area."

"Fat lot of good it did us," said Chief Tucker.

"Wait," said Curtis, putting out a hand. He felt like he could see where Frankie was going.

Frankie took the picture of Miranda O'Connell off the wall and placed it on the desk. "If we take out Miranda O'Connell," she said, "then patterns begin to emerge. They were all on the outskirts of town, in areas where they shouldn't have been, drinking or possibly doing drugs."

"What about the fourth body?" said Chief Tucker. "We pulled four bodies from that pond. Are you saying we just ignore the fourth body?"

Frankie sighed, yet she looked proud. "I should have seen it earlier. None of you were in the room when the O'Connells came to identify their daughter. All the others took one look, and even in that rotten, desecrated state, they were able to identify which body belonged to their daughters instantly. The O'Connells hesitated. They waited too long, and I think it was more Dr. Novak's reactions and subtle hints toward the unclaimed body we wanted them to pick that made their decision for them."

"You're saying they picked the wrong body?" said Tucker. "Why?"

"Because we wanted them to," said Frankie, "and they wanted closure. We wanted clues, and they wanted to know that their daughter's suffering was over. They would rather she was dead, and nothing more could happen to her than that she was still in the kidnapper's grasp."

Tucker put his hands in the air, as though he was at a complete loss.

"I think the fourth body is someone else," said Frankie. "Another victim of the killer from somewhere else that he hid in the same spot." She paused as though for dramatic effect. "And I think Miranda O'Connell is still alive."

CHAPTER 38

THE ENTIRE ROOM FELL SILENT.

For a few moments, the only sound was the wind outside the windows. Curtis was first to recover. He looked at the board, tracing the connections and trying to find a flaw in Frankie's logic. There was none he could see. It wouldn't stand up in court, but it was a starting point. That was all they needed right now.

Taking Miranda O'Connell out changed everything. Patterns started emerging, and some semblance of order began to appear on the wall in front of them.

Chief Tucker began to pace back and forth across the room, mumbling to himself like an insane mathematician. Trevor and Monica just sat there, looking like two kids in a class where the material was so far above their heads they just nodded along.

"So what now?" said Curtis. "What does that leave us with?"

Frankie glanced back at the wall. "Start with the obvious and work our way out from there. All of these girls were underage, all were drinking on the night of their respective kidnappings. It makes sense that the two are connected. Who works at a bar and has served prison time?"

Curtis frowned. "Bobby Randall? You think he's the killer?"

Frankie shrugged. "It would explain why he pushed you toward Marino. He was trying to distract you. He might be our best suspect."

Curtis sighed, trying to find the flaw in the logic. "Okay," he said after a pause. He checked his watch. "I don't see him as a killer, but we can talk to him. He'll probably be home now. Trevor, can you get his address? I'll talk to him. Have cars set up outside if he tries to run."

Chief Tucker said, "You got it."

Curtis looked around the room. "Anyone else have anything to say?"

No one said anything, so they stood and walked out to their cars. Monica was tasked with calling the judge.

They stopped by the judge's house and pick up the arrest and search warrants.

They drove through the dark and windy night to Bobby Randall's home. It was only a block from Randall's Tavern, and the light from the television could be seen through the blinds.

Curtis knocked on the door. Bobby answered a few moments later, wearing a white t-shirt and sweatpants.

"What are you doing here, Curtis?" he said. He looked past Curtis to the police cars parked along the road. He frowned. "Did you find something?"

"Bobby," said Curtis, feeling uneasy. He knew Frankie's logic was sound and that they had no other suspects, but his gut was telling him this was wrong. "Why did you tell me about Marino?"

Bobby shrugged. "I thought you deserved to know. You were in danger." He opened his eyes wide, as though a light had just gone on in his head. "You think I did it? You think I killed those girls?"

"Did you?" Curtis tried to look as sympathetic as possible. "We can sort this all out if you just tell me what happened. Was it an accident?"

"No! I didn't do anything! Why would you think I did it, Curtis? I helped you! I fucking helped you!"

"I'm sorry," said Curtis. "If you're innocent, I need you to come with me now, and we can clear this up." Curtis held up the two warrants. "Bobby Randall, this is a warrant to search your home in connection to the murders of Darcy Oberman, Harriet Matheson, Ashley Hagerty, and Miranda O'Connell."

He wondered absentmindedly when they would reveal to the O'Connells that their daughter was alive. They had decided to keep that information secret, but every moment which passed was another in which the parents were grieving a body that wasn't their daughter.

"What?" said Bobby, grabbing the warrant and reading it. "Curtis... Come on, you know me."

"Come with us to the station, and we'll get this all sorted out."

"You've got to be fucking kidding me." Bobby stared at the warrant for a few more moments. When he spoke, his voice was soft and defeated. "Curtis, can you do me a favor?"

Curtis shrugged. "What?"

"Don't tell anyone about this. I've had enough difficulty rebuilding my life without needing to be arrested again. If people think I killed those girls, that could be the end for me."

Curtis nodded. "I promise."

"Okay."

Bobby and Curtis walked out to the waiting police car. Curtis read him his rights as they walked, but Bobby wasn't listening.

Bobby climbed into the back seat of the car without saying a word.

"You know," said Frankie once Bobby was secured in the back of the car, "I keep expecting Natasha to show up, but I guess she's not coming, huh?"

"I guess not." Curtis glanced at the back seat. Bobby was staring out at the neighborhood around them. "Let's leave Bobby at the station for a bit and let him stew overnight while we search his house. Keep him separate from Nolowinski. In the morning we'll be well rested, and he'll be ready to talk if there's anything else."

Frankie thought for a moment, then nodded. "Unless we come up with anyone else as a suspect or something else happens."

"Agreed."

They climbed into the car and drove back toward the jail. Curtis looked at Bobby in the rearview mirror. He didn't look like a killer or show any signs of guilt.

Then again, serial killers had a disturbing tendency of looking like normal, everyday people.

CHAPTER 39

CURTIS SAT IN THEIR MOTEL ROOM, LISTENING TO THE GENTLE breathing of Frankie's sleep. Her cross necklace had fallen to one side and rested on the pillow. Curtis had never understood her faith but had also never questioned it. Whatever kept people going through the hardships of life was their business as far as he was concerned. As long as no one was dragging him to church or forcing their beliefs down his throat, they could believe whatever they wanted.

His phone rang. It was a call he'd been expecting. He stood and walked out to the balcony, which overlooked the highway. The streetlights illuminated the road below him as a transport truck thundered past.

"Hey," he said, leaning on the railing. "How are you doing?"

"I'm doing well," said Melanie, sounding tired. "How about yourself?"

"I've been better. Seen some things I'd prefer not to."

"You catch the killer yet?"

Curtis sighed. "Not yet. We have someone in custody we think might be the guy, but I have a bad feeling about it. I don't think it's the guy. It's nice to hear your voice."

"Thanks, sweetie."

"Tell me about your day. I need a distraction."

"Well," said Melanie, "this weekend has actually been tough for us. We have a big project with Ford, so we've been working all weekend trying to get that prepared. It's mostly print ads, you know, newspapers and magazines, but there's also a possibility we'll get to start doing some television ads if they like these."

"That's awesome."

"Yeah, I'm proud of them," said Melanie. "It's been a bit of a nightmare with morning sickness and all that."

Curtis smiled and listened as Melanie continued talking about her life, her worries, and her concerns. It seemed so small compared to the life and death issues he was dealing with, yet at the same time that tether to the real world, a world where his only concern was what color to paint the nursery, kept him happy and sane.

It was also what reminded him of his promise to go back.

About an hour later, Melanie realized it was almost midnight and hung up, citing that she needed to be at work the next morning. After saying their "I love you"s and the usual promise that he would return to her, Curtis was left standing on the balcony with his phone in his hand. He stared straight out over the highway, watching the transport trucks thunder past every few minutes. In the distance, he could see the lights of downtown Blind River.

He took a deep breath. He thought of the family he would soon have. That was what he was fighting for.

Curtis saw the logic in arresting Bobby Randall, but there was something about it that just didn't work. Curtis stared up at the half moon, trying to figure out what was bugging him.

He sighed and went back into the motel room.

CHAPTER 40

KENDRA MATHESON SLOUCHED OVER THE BAR, COUNTRY MUSIC blasting behind her.

She hated country music. The rest of the week Sally's Bar and Grill was a respectable establishment where she could get whatever she wanted, but tonight it was filled with cowboy boots, cowboy hats, and way too much plaid. There was a country band on stage and a dance floor filled with untalented dancers attempting to square dance.

Kendra waved a hand to Sally, the bartender, and shook her empty glass. Normally, Sally would have cut her off by this point, but what Kendra had been through that day bypassed any such limits. She'd identified her sister's dead body that day. If anyone deserved a drink, it was her.

Sally poured her another drink and half-heartedly told her to slow down, before giving up.

"You look like you could use some company."

Kendra looked up to see a man sitting beside her wearing a black button-down shirt. The only country thing about him was an ill-fitting cowboy hat on top of his head. It took her a moment to recognize Nate Williams out of his prison guard uniform, but when she did, she smiled. "Hey, Nate," she said. "Not working tonight?"

Nate took that as an invitation and slid onto the seat beside her. "I'm heading over to the prison in an hour or so, actually. I have a night shift. I can't drink for that reason. One of my buddies invited me out for a bit." He suddenly became somber. "I heard what happened today. I'm sorry."

Kendra nodded and finished her drink. She vaguely remembered Nate being married to that Mackley detective woman, and that the separation hadn't been civil. She even heard that Detective Mackley had fired a gun at him, but hadn't gotten any confirmation on that rumor. "Thanks."

She wobbled back and forth and had to steady herself against the bar.

Nate put a hand on her shoulder and said, "Come on, let's get you home. You're drunk."

"I'm fine."

"No," he said sternly. "Let's go."

Kendra looked at the empty cup in her hand and nodded.

Nate took Kendra under his arms and nodded to Sally, who seemed thankful she didn't have to do it.

They walked through the bar, weaving around a few teenage girls with plaid shirts tied in the front to reveal their cleavage. Nate's eyes strayed just a bit, and Kendra laughed, forcing him to return his focus to her.

He smiled at her, and Kendra wondered why he'd never made a move on her. They'd known each other for almost fifteen years. For a time, she'd wondered if he was gay, but his brief marriage to Detective Mackley and his wandering eyes had killed that idea.

They stepped outside. The feeling of a storm was thick in the air, and the sky was dark, the stars and the moon invisible behind the clouds.

"My car's over there," said Kendra, taking a lunging step.

"No," said Nate. "You're drunk. I'll drive you home. Pick up the car tomorrow. It's this way."

They walked across the parking lot, away from the area illuminated by streetlights and the fluorescent sign above the bar. The music faded as they walked toward the edge of the parking lot.

"Excuse me," said a voice in the darkness. "Can you give me some help?"

"Who's there?" said Nate, taking a cautious step toward the figure in the darkness. Nate took a few tentative steps, leaving Kendra to lean against an adjacent car.

"I need some help with my car," said the figure. "Damn thing won't start."

Kendra closed one eye, trying to focus on the figure, then opened them wide when she recognized the man. "Oh hey," she said, "how are you?"

Upon hearing her calm question, Nate turned back to the man and recognized him as well. He smiled. "What seems to be the issue?"

"I don't know," said the man. "There's a weird smell coming from the engine. You think you could check it out?"

"Sure," said Nate, rolling up his sleeves and walking over. "Where was the smell coming from?"

"Right there," said the man, pointing deep into the engine.

Kendra leaned against the car, watching them. She was

the first to see the gun the man took from his right pocket. He looked back at Kendra and held a finger to his lips.

Kendra frowned, her drunk mind so far behind that she couldn't react.

"Back here, you mean?" said Nate, leaning deep into the engine. "I can't see anything."

"It's around there somewhere." The figure took a suppressor out of his pocket and attached it to the end of the gun. Kendra stared at him through her haze. The loud music from the bar blocked out any other sound.

The man put the gun to the back of Nate's head and fired once. The blood from his forehead covered the front of the engine. A little bit sprayed through the gap at the bottom of the hood and onto the front windshield. Nate spasmed for just a moment and made a low moaning sound before becoming still on top of the engine. The figure then lifted the gun and aimed it at Kendra.

"If you make a sound," he said, "you're next."

Kendra nodded and pushed herself against the car.

The man grabbed the back of Nate's shirt and yanked him off the engine and onto the ground. A spurt of blood came from his forehead as his dead body fell.

The man kept his gun trained on Kendra as he grabbed Nate's lifeless hand and effortlessly dragged him across the pavement to the trunk of the car.

He opened the trunk and lifted Nate's body inside. By the time Kendra thought to run, the trunk was closed, and the gun was back pointing at her.

"Maybe don't drink so much next time," said the man as he walked around to the front of the car. He glanced over his shoulder when the front door of the bar opened. A man and a woman walked out, laughing at one another, the girl leaning her head on the man's shoulder. They never looked toward the location of the shooting, nor did they turn in their direction. In less than a minute, they were gone, and Kendra was back alone with the man. She could have screamed, but the gun in her face made her mute with fear.

The figure walked to the front of the car and closed the hatch, concealing all except for the blood which had sprayed onto the front windshield. He took a cloth out of his pocket, spat on it, and used it to wipe it off. What remained when he was finished could easily be confused with dirt.

"Come with me," he said, walking over to Kendra and putting the gun in her ribs. "I don't want to hurt you."

Kendra raised her hands as they walked, leaving the car where Nate's body was stored behind them. It only occurred to her now that the car had been a plant, an intentional diversion.

"You killed Harriet," she said as the truth dawned on her. "You killed my sister and threw her in that river."

The man laughed softly. "She begged for her life, you know? She put up a fight. Who would have guessed I would get to kill both the Matheson sisters?"

Kendra said nothing. She willed her body to fight back, to turn and attack the man who had killed her sister and was going to kill her. She could run. She could get away and tell everyone who the killer was.

Despite her begging thoughts, her body refused to listen, and they got to the car where she was being led without any struggle. The figure opened the trunk and grabbed a roll of duct tape. He held it out to her. "Tape your mouth shut."

Kendra took the tape and obeyed, the barrel of the gun

holding her in a trance she couldn't break. She was instructed to tape her feet together and did so. She handed back the tape and held out her hands, per his instructions, and had her wrists bound together. At that moment, she realized she was beyond help.

She tried to wail, but her cries were muffled by the tape covering her mouth. The man opened the trunk and gestured for her to get in, the gun still pointed at her chest. Kendra turned her head back toward the bar, which was too far away for even an unmuffled scream. The music had become dimmed, and she could only barely see the lights from the bar.

"I don't have all night," said the man. "I can kill you like I did Nate and get someone else. There are other people I can grab. Get in the trunk."

Kendra was certain she was going to die, but even in that moment of abject terror, of absolute certainty that this was the end of her life, she couldn't gather the courage to run. She cursed her own cowardice, her own weakness, her own inability to fix her own problems.

With tears running down her face, she fell into the trunk. Her kidnapper threw her legs in after her. The trunk slammed closed over her, sentencing her to darkness.

She tried to wail again but heard nothing but the driver's door opening and closing and the engine starting.

CHAPTER 41

HARRY OCHRE RUBBED HIS EYES. HE'D BEEN AT THE PRISON FOR nine hours and was exhausted. He couldn't wait to get home. Martha, his wife, was making a roast, her specialty. He'd been thinking about it all day.

"Ochre!"

Harry looked up and saw another guard approaching him. "What?"

"Warden wants to see you," said the guard.

The guard turned and walked away. Harry let out a sigh. He hoped he hadn't drawn the short straw.

Nate hadn't shown up to work yet, and he had been aware of the possibility he would have to take Nate's shift. A common issue in prisons was a lack of guards, due to the difficulty of the job. It was impossible to tell if someone would be able to do it until they were in the thick of it. If they quit, the entire training process would have to restart.

Harry walked through the prison, ignoring the jeers from the prisoners. After a certain point, it became the quiet criminals who unnerved him. That was the feeling he had whenever he passed Sam Marino's cell. The former crime boss looked up from his novel for just a moment, looked Harry in the eyes, then returned to his book with a smirk, as though he knew something Harry didn't.

Harry left the cell block and took the elevator up to the warden's office. When he entered, Warden Thompson stood from his desk and walked around to shake Harry's hand. The warden treated every person coming into his office as if he was a visiting dignitary, something that had always bothered Harry. They took their seats, and the warden became all business.

"You know I hate to do this," said Thompson, taking his seat, "but you need to stay late. Nate Williams hasn't shown up, and we can't reach him. You'll just need to be here until he shows up."

Harry sighed. "I didn't realize it was my turn."

Thompson held up his palms and shrugged.

"I have a home-cooked meal waiting at home," said Harry. "My wife's been working on it all day."

"I wish there was something I could do, but there isn't," said Thompson. "When Williams shows up, you can leave right away."

Thompson stood and walked past Harry, grabbing his coat. "I'll be at home. Let me know if there's any reason for me to come in."

Harry sighed. "Yes, sir."

He stood and followed Thompson out of the office. They rode the elevator down together in silence. They exited at different floors, and the last Harry saw of Thompson was an apologetic expression through the closing doors of the elevator.

Harry sighed and walked to the break room, stopping only to let another guard know he was taking a break and he'd be back to take Nate's shift.

Harry was getting concerned about Nate. He wasn't someone who missed a shift without reason under any circumstances. With everything going on in Blind River, Harry felt uneasy. The visits from the FBI agents had been some of the most nerve-wracking moments he'd had on this job, and that was even without Nate's ex-wife being involved. Harry didn't know what had caused the split, but he would have bet a lot of money it wasn't amicable.

He grabbed a bottle of water from the break room and took out his cell phone. He dialed his wife and sighed as it rang.

"Hello?" said Martha, the sounds of bubbling water and a television playing in the background.

"Hey, it's me."

"Why are you calling? You should be almost home."

"Nate never showed for his shift."

There was a long silence, then Martha said, "You're going to miss dinner, aren't you?"

"Looks like it," said Harry, "unless Nate shows in the next few hours."

Martha sighed. "I'll leave your food in the fridge. Microwave it when you get in."

"Thanks. Martha?"

"Yeah?"

"I'm sorry," said Harry. "I know you worked hard on this."

"I understand."

The call ended. Harry cursed silently to himself and slid his phone into his pocket. He checked himself in the bathroom mirror before heading out for a circuit of the cell block.

The good thing about a night shift was that there was little to do. They made sure everyone was in their cells, then shut off the lights. After that, they did a circuit every hour or so, but nothing ever happened. The night shift was mostly spent in the break room with the other guards.

Harry joined the others, and they did a circuit, ensuring everyone was in their cells. Harry avoided Sam Marino's gaze as he passed the cell, knowing he would see nothing but an eerie calmness in Marino's eyes, something he didn't want on his mind that night.

They finished their rounds and shut off the lights. The prison went dark except for the lights which illuminated the walkways so the guards could see where they were going.

Harry walked into the break room and took a deep breath. No matter how long he worked at the prison, there was always a feeling of relief when he walked through that door.

He and the other guards spent the next hour relaxing and playing cards, making jokes about what had happened to Nate. The prevailing theory was that his penchant for risqué women had finally caught up to him and he was tied to a bed somewhere, a gag in his mouth. Monica Mackley had been a break from that rule. That was the reason Harry hadn't been surprised when it fell apart.

When Nate was back at work, they would give him hell for his mistake. No one mentioned the possibility that Nate wouldn't be working again.

At ten, they stood and exited the room to do another round.

Harry sighed, his eyes drooping and his focus waning. He'd been working for twelve hours, eight more than any of the others.

They walked through the prison, checking that everyone was asleep in their cells. It was odd, thought Harry as he walked, the way prisoners lose their liberties. They were told when to go to the bathroom, sleep, work and relax. They didn't have the freedoms most people took for granted. One bad decision could take it all away.

It wasn't until he was almost done with his circuit that Harry got the creeping sensation something wasn't quite right. He felt a cold sweat run down his neck.

He glanced back toward Sam Marino's cell, fifty feet behind him, and saw that the cell door was closed. He had avoided looking inside the cell when he passed. He took a deep breath and turned forward. The break room was less than twenty feet away. There was nothing to be concerned about. His fatigue was just playing tricks on him.

He gasped as the sharpened toothbrush came down into his back, sliding between his ribs and into his right lung. He grabbed at his chest as he fell to the floor, the toothbrush protruding from his back.

He tried to cry out as he felt his lungs fill with blood, but no sounds came from his mouth. He looked around and saw none of the other guards.

He felt a shadow leaning over him. A knee pushed into his back, accelerating the rate at which he was internally bleeding.

"Guess you're a little tired," said Sam Marino above him, in that same whisper Harry found so disconcerting. "Guess this shift was a little too long for you. You never locked my cell. The entire prison system is a mess, isn't it? You're so understaffed that they hire retards like you, and they can't even afford some automatic locking mechanisms. Pathetic. What is this? The eighties?"

Marino laughed softly.

Harry tried to respond, but once again nothing came from his mouth except a spray of blood. He managed to look to his right, toward the cells. The other prisoners had awoken and were watching the events unfold. Not one cried out for help, not one did anything, not one met Harry's pleading eyes.

This was Marino's prison.

Harry flailed for the taser at his waist, the excuse they were given instead of a gun. Marino's foot came down on his wrist hard.

"I'll be taking these," said Marino, grabbing both the taser and the keys from Harry's belt. "Thanks for your hospitality."

The pressure disappeared from Harry's back. The patter of footsteps receded away, toward the exit. He tried to cry out again, but only a strained gurgling came from his mouth.

A guard rounded the corner in front of him, walking and whistling, spinning his keys around his finger. The moment he caught sight of Harry lying face first in a puddle of his own blood, he grabbed his radio and sprinted towards Harry.

"Man down," he shouted into his radio. "Prisoner escaping. Marino is out of his cell. Get medical attention. Over."

Harry listened to the replies through the radio on his shoulder, but the words seemed to get further and further away.

The other guards responded as quickly as they could. The sentries on the walls confirmed that they'd prevent Marino from getting past the walls. Another said he would get a medical team. Harry didn't think either would succeed. He was sure Marino was going to escape, and he was going to die.

Marino wouldn't have done this if he didn't think he could get away with it.

The guard put a hand on Harry's back, reaching for the toothbrush, then decided to leave it in. He patted Harry gently on the back.

"You'll be fine," he said, his voice a trained calm. "The doctors will get here, and everything will be fine. You will be fine."

Harry didn't believe him. "Tell my wife I love her."

"Tell her yourself," said the guard. "You have plenty of time. Save your energy."

Harry smiled as his head slumped against the ground. He wouldn't make it home in time for dinner.

CHAPTER 42

CURTIS LEANED OVER THE BALCONY RAILING AND WATCHED THE sunrise. Frankie was inside the motel room, talking on the phone with someone. It was probably Director Johnson.

Curtis had no illusions about Johnson's worries, and he knew Frankie was giving the director updates. He understood. He would have done the same.

Hopefully, Natasha and Bobby would be ready to talk. If they were lucky, they would be able to get signed confessions before lunch and be back in Manhattan by dinner. Curtis could take a few days off and spend time with Melanie.

The door behind him opened and Frankie stepped out, looking worried. Curtis knew without asking that they wouldn't be getting home.

"What happened?" he asked.

"Marino escaped from prison and killed a guard," said Frankie blankly.

Curtis turned back from her, the words rattling around the inside of his head. He gripped the banister harder. "Which guard?" he asked.

"Harry Ochre. Sharpened toothbrush through the back, punctured his lung. He died of internal bleeding."

Curtis took a deep breath. "Where's Marino?"

"He got away. He's probably trying to put as much distance between us as possible."

Curtis felt an anger rising within him. "What did Johnson say?"

"It's not our responsibility," said Frankie. "We focus entirely on the missing girls. Don't even think about Marino. Johnson's sending a separate team to help the police recapture Marino, a team that specializes in prisoner retrieval."

Curtis nodded, gripping the railing. He had put Marino in prison. Marino wanted his blood. Until that moment it hadn't mattered. Now Marino was out in the world, somewhere he could get revenge.

"I hate this fucking town," said Curtis, walking back into the motel room. He would listen to Johnson, but he knew, given the opportunity, he would put a bullet into Marino's head.

The immensity of what had happened followed them through the town to the police station. Outside the station was a ragged band of protesters holding signs proclaiming that the police were unable to protect them and that Sam Marino was going to destroy the town they had worked so hard to rebuild. Others shouted that they wanted a return to Marino rule.

They were no threat, however, without Natasha's ability to focus the crowd's anger. The protesters didn't react to Curtis and Frankie when they arrived.

Chief Tucker welcomed them into his office, where Trevor was already waiting. He explained that Monica was back at the hospital to give the nurse a break. Curtis nodded. He wondered whether she'd gotten in contact with Nate to ask about Harry and Marino's escape.

They sat across from Chief Tucker, who looked as though he hadn't slept at all the previous night. A secretary came into the office with a steaming cup of coffee, and he thanked her, downing the black coffee in a single gulp.

He let out a long sigh, then looked at the two FBI agents. "You already know about the jailbreak?"

Frankie nodded. "How did it happen? Aren't there failsafes?"

"Nate Williams never showed up for work last night," said Tucker. "We still don't know where he is. Harry Ochre took his shift. He was working for twelve hours straight and made a mistake. He didn't lock Marino's cell. Marino attacked him while he was alone. It's never happened before. The guards weren't properly trained. Marino got into the control console for the front gate, put a gun to the guard's head, and forced him to open both gates. One of the snipers got a shot off but missed. You can only do so much training. The real thing will always be a different beast."

Frankie nodded. "Director Johnson is sending an FBI team who specializes in prisoner retrieval. We focus on the murdered girls."

Tucker rubbed his eyes. "With you two, the retrieval team for the pond, and now this, we may as well set up an FBI field office."

Frankie smiled at him. "Bobby Randall is still in the jail?"

"Yeah. He's eaten and gotten some rest, but he's getting a little pent up. I think he'll talk."

"Great."

Curtis turned and looked back at Trevor, who smiled awkwardly. He looked uncomfortable, as though he'd never thought he'd have to deal with a situation like this. Curtis once again tried to gather some recollection of Trevor from high school, but once again came up empty.

"What about Williams?" said Curtis, turning back to Tucker. "Where the hell is he?"

"He was at Sally's Bar and Grill last night," said Chief Tucker. "He left half an hour before his shift was going to start. We don't know what happened next. We have a team looking right now."

"Is it possible Marino planned that to escape?"

Tucker shrugged. "I don't see how. It would be an extremely convoluted plan. I think Marino saw an opportunity and took it."

Curtis nodded. He looked at Trevor. "You find Nate Williams. It might be related, and it might not be, but we need to know."

Trevor nodded and stood, then walked past them and out of the station.

Curtis and Frankie made sure Chief Tucker was clear on their plan and walked to the jail.

The two police officers tasked with guarding it lounged outside the jail cells and admitted them when they approached. Three of the four cells had been newly occupied over the previous twenty-four hours.

Ken Hagerty was still slouched in his cell. He looked up with pleading eyes when Curtis passed.

"The deal's still available," said Curtis. "Confess, and we'll let you go. Your bail hearing is set for tomorrow morning."

Ken glared at him, and Curtis ignored him. Across from

Ken was Natasha. Somehow her complete calmness was the most unnerving thing in the jail. She looked too calm and collected for someone who had spent the night in jail. Even her hair was only mildly messy.

The third cell was occupied by the newest arrival, the most worried and the most panicked. Bobby Randall paced back and forth in his cell, muttering to himself. He had heavy bags under his eyes, and his clothes were wrinkled and disheveled. He was either an extremely good actor, or he was exhibiting behaviors inconsistent with the actions of the killer.

"Bobby, come with us," said Frankie, opening the cell door with keys she'd gotten from the guards.

Bobby was led through the jail. Ken jumped to his feet as he walked past, his eyes wide and filled with fury. Curtis could imagine what was taking place.

Bobby would have lied to Ken about why he'd been arrested. Ken didn't know the person suspected of killing his daughter was in the cell right next to him. Now that the FBI agents were leading him away, though, the pieces came together in his head.

On the other side of the cell block, Natasha kept grinning, as though she was watching an amusing spectacle. Curtis could almost see the story she was writing in her mind. She was probably even thinking that this story might catapult her to something greater, the inside story of a serial killer investigation.

Ken started to shout at them when they exited the jail, but the door cut him off.

They led Bobby to an interview room. He sat in the chair opposite the one-way mirror. It was a conscious decision not to cuff him. He would be more willing to talk if he didn't feel like a prisoner.

Frankie Mirandized him, and they took their seats.

"So, Bobby," said Curtis. "Have anything you want to tell us?"

"I swear I didn't do anything," said Bobby. "I had nothing to do with whatever happened to those girls."

"Let's begin with the girls," said Curtis, taking control of the interview. "Did you know the girls who died? Ashley? Harriet? Darcy? Miranda?"

Bobby avoided his gaze. "I knew them."

"How did you know them?"

"They were just around. I knew their parents."

"Were they at the bar?"

"Yes, I mean, sometimes."

"Bobby. You need to be honest with me right now. Confessing to a lesser crime will get you off multiple murder charges. You should know that you're the only suspect right now."

Bobby looked at Frankie as though asking for help, but her blank expression didn't waver. He turned back to Curtis, hesitated, turned back to Frankie. "I gave them some alcohol, okay? That's all. I gave them beer, then they went on their way. They wanted to pay me. Instead, I made them promise they would stay safe. I didn't give them enough to get drunk, just enough to have a good time. If I hadn't, they would have gotten it somewhere else."

Curtis nodded. "Kids will get alcohol no matter what."

"Exactly. That's all I did."

"With which of the girls?"

"All of them, except for Miranda O'Connell. She didn't take any. She didn't drink, as far as I know."

Curtis grinned.

Bobby fell back into his chair, his smile disappearing, as though he knew he'd made a mistake but didn't know what it was.

"I'm going to tell you something we haven't released to the public yet," said Curtis. "We believe Miranda O'Connell is still alive."

Bobby frowned for a moment, processing the new information. His eyes opened wide. "That doesn't mean anything."

"It seems oddly convenient, don't you think?"

Bobby paused for a moment. "I want a lawyer. I should never have let you take me in here without a lawyer. The guys in prison told me to get a lawyer as soon as I was arrested, but I trusted you, Curtis. I didn't need to tell you about Marino, but I did. And why did I do that? Because I was your friend, and I wanted to help save those girls, you fucking dick."

Curtis stood without another word. "You'll get your lawyer. Then we'll be back. But before then you'll have to be put back in the cells with Ken Hagerty. He'll know exactly why you're here."

Bobby looked nervous, but he didn't cave.

Frankie stood as well. They left the room and told one of the officers to get Bobby a lawyer.

"M.E.?" said Frankie.

"May as well," said Curtis.

They walked through the police station, passing by Matt Oberman and Joe Hagerty, who nodded politely as they passed. Both looked serious.

Once they were out of earshot, Frankie said, "It must be

hard on them, being in the middle of all of this with their families so involved. They can't even take time off because we need all the manpower we can get."

"I know," said Curtis, looking over his shoulder as the two officers walked toward the jail, toward where the man accused of brutally murdering their loved ones was being held.

Curtis and Frankie found Dr. Novak in the Medical Examiner's Office, reading a Tess Gerritsen novel. She looked up when they entered and dog-eared her page.

"I was taking a break," she said. "I've got most of the autopsies done."

"What have you got?" said Frankie.

"Not much," said Dr. Novak, standing and walking out of the room, the FBI agents behind her. "The bodies are too decomposed to find much. I've received the medical files on the four girls, but thus far those haven't been much help. There are two things I've discovered which I think are important. The first is that all four bodies showed signs of frostbite."

"Frostbite?" said Curtis as they walked into the room where the bodies were covered in sheets. "Frostbite from what?"

Novak shrugged. "Anything from having been dunked into a bath of ice cubes to being in a cold climate. I did a semester working in the Northern Arctic during college, and that's the only other time I've seen anything like this."

"That's odd." Curtis made a mental note of it. "What about blood types? Have you matched those?"

Novak shook her head. "Not yet. We have the positive IDs, so it didn't seem urgent. Is there something I should know?"

Frankie nodded. "We don't think the body identified as Miranda O'Connell is actually her. We believe it's another victim of the killer whose body he hid in the same place. You understand we can't let this get out to the public."

Novak processed this information, then said, "That explains the second thing I was going to tell you."

Frankie raised an eyebrow. "Which is?"

Dr. Novak walked over to the body which had been identified as Miranda O'Connell. She pulled back the sheet to reveal the disintegrated flesh of the face. "This body is different from the others in two ways. The first is that it is far more decomposed. It's been in the water longer than the others by a significant margin."

Frankie nodded. "And the other thing?"

"She's older," said Novak. "She has a more mature body shape. I would put her in her mid to late thirties at the time of death. There's also signs of a C-section."

Curtis frowned. "That doesn't fit the targets. Why would the killer attack someone so different than his usual targets?"

"Maybe they were all crimes of opportunity," said Frankie.

Novak crossed her arms. "Then where's Miranda O'Connell?"

"Our working theory is she's still alive," said Curtis. "She ran away from her overbearing parents. The crime scene is too distinct. If we take her out, patterns start emerging."

"We had a few case studies like that at school." Novak sighed. "I'll do the blood typing tests and see if I can get a confirmation that this isn't Miranda O'Connell. I heard you made an arrest?"

Frankie frowned. "Where'd you hear that?"

"One of the officers. Oberman and Hagerty were talking about it."

"Don't let that get out," said Frankie sternly. "It's supposed to be private."

"Sure thing, Agent." Novak had begun the sentence with a sarcastic tone but tempered it as she continued, as though remembering who she was talking to. She cleared her throat and in a more serious tone said, "I'll get to work."

CHAPTER 43

Trevor walked up the Mathesons' front walk. The two officers assigned to finding Nate Williams followed.

Trevor wished he didn't have to come here. Oscar Matheson had been through enough already, but Sally from Sally's Bar and Grill had been adamant that a drunk Kendra Matheson had left the bar on the arm of Nate Williams. No one had seen them after that, and so the only logical conclusion was either they'd gone back to the Mathesons' house and lost track of time, or something had happened.

Trevor knocked and heard a grumble from inside. The door flew open. Oscar Matheson didn't look drunk. He looked scared and angry.

"Where's Kendra?" he said.

"Mr. Matheson, I'm Detective Trevor Marshall. We're looking for Kendra."

"Where is she?"

"We don't know. She was with Nate Williams last night, and we can't find either of them."

"She isn't dead?" said Oscar.

"No, Mr. Matheson. She's not dead. We just need to find her."

"Thank God." Oscar fell to his knees. Tears began running down his face. "I was so worried."

"Mr. Matheson." Trevor put a hand on his shoulder. He looked up at Trevor through tear soaked eyes. "When was the last time you saw Kendra? We need to speak to her."

"I haven't seen her since yesterday."

"Do you know where she was going after that?"

Oscar shook his head. "She doesn't tell me anything."

"Thank you, we'll be in touch, Mr. Matheson."

"If you find her, please tell me."

"We'll let you know."

"No matter what?"

"No matter what."

Oscar nodded, as though a weight had been lifted from his shoulders.

CHAPTER 44

NATASHA LEANED BACK AGAINST THE CELL WALL AND WATCHED as Bobby Randall was led past. She tried to commit everything to memory, knowing she had a front row seat to a story that could launch her career. The Blind River Observer had never been good enough. It had never given her the reach or the power she deserved.

Ken was in his cell, his face a mask of fury that only a grieving father could have achieved. He remained silent as the guards led Bobby Randall to the cell adjacent to his, locked him in, then walked out. Bobby Randall looked petrified.

Natasha grinned as the guards disappeared through the door. She caught a glimpse of Officers Joe Hagerty and Matt Oberman on the other side. They were talking with the guards outside.

Ken took a deep breath, as though readying his onslaught of insults and attacks on the man who had killed his daughter. He leaned through the bars and looked sideways toward the cell where Bobby sat.

Natasha smiled. Something was going to happen, and she was going to have a front row seat.

CHAPTER 45

CURTIS AND FRANKIE WERE LEAVING THE STATION WHEN Bobby's lawyer arrived. He was scrawny, and his suit was too big. He introduced himself as Thomas Goldstein.

Frankie explained the situation to him. While they were talking, Curtis's phone rang. He picked it up and motioned to Frankie that he needed to take it. She nodded and continued talking to Goldstein while Curtis walked away and answered the call.

"Hey, Monica," he answered. "What's up?"

There was no response except for a mild sobbing and the sound of footsteps in the background. Curtis could feel a lump growing on his heart. Somehow he already knew what was going to be said.

There was the sound of Monica taking a deep breath as if to prepare herself.

"Dad's dead."

CHAPTER 46

CURTIS WALKED THROUGH THE HALLS OF THE HOSPITAL IN A trance. The nurses moved to avoid him. Somehow, in the back of his mind, he was thinking about how the hall would be much nicer if it was blue instead of a gloomy beige.

He passed by the room where Zach O'Reilly was and nodded to Mr. O'Reilly, sitting beside the bed. Zach was awake and gave him a smile. Apparently, Ken Hagerty wouldn't be tried for murder. Just kidnapping and attempted murder.

Curtis turned into the room. Monica was sitting in the chair below their father's bed, her head bowed, motionless. A doctor beside the bed introduced himself as Doctor Larson. He explained that Gordon Mackley had had another stroke just as he had passed the twenty-four-hour mark. His heart had been unable to deal with it. They had tried unsuccessfully to resuscitate him. Curtis listened with a blank expression, unable to process the information.

He couldn't take his eyes off his father, lying in bed, his body motionless. Even though he'd seen his father sleeping before, there was a lack of motion now which seemed impossible. He was so still.

The images of the bodies of the missing girls desecrated and rotting from their time in the pond, charged into his mind. He couldn't help but imagine his father below the ground, his body slowly returning to the soil. He always knew when he looked at dead bodies that they'd been a person with hopes, fears, feelings, loves and hates, but it was entirely different when it was someone he was close to.

"Can you give us a minute?" he said to the doctor.

Larson nodded. "A nurse will be outside the door. I'm sorry for your loss."

"Thanks."

When Larson was gone, Curtis fell into a chair beside Monica, and they looked at the once great Gordon Mackley. Now he was just flesh and bone, losing the essence that had made him who he was. This was where Frankie would have said something about Gordon being in a better place now, but Curtis didn't really believe that.

One thing was for certain, however. The world in which they were living had just become a little worse.

"What happened?" said Curtis.

"Me and Dad were talking," said Monica. "We were talking about Nate."

"Your ex? Why?"

Monica sighed. "Nothing."

"What?"

"Nate and I started fighting a lot once we were married. I pulled my gun on him once when I was angry. He came at me, and I fired at him. I missed, and he thought it was a warning shot. It wasn't. I was trying to shoot him. I just missed. He moved out the next day."

Curtis nodded along, thinking of the bullet hole in Monica's house, feeling as though nothing could shock him at this point. "Nate never told anyone?"

"Not that I know of." Monica took a deep breath. "I stayed at dad's last night. When I came here, he looked fine. We talked. He was in and out of focus. The doctor came in this morning and said he would be fine."

Curtis nodded. "He just died? Fine one minute and gone the next?"

Monica nodded.

"He deserved better."

"He wouldn't have complained."

Curtis smiled, wondering what Gordon Mackley would say to them now. Probably something along the lines of "suck it up and move on."

Not yet, thought Curtis.

Monica leaned over and put her head on Curtis's shoulder.

They sat there, letting the weight of the world rest on their shoulders. For that moment, it felt like their entire family was back together. Curtis, Monica, Josh, their parents Gordon and Barbara. They were together, like they had always dreamed.

Just for that moment.

CHAPTER 47

TREVOR MARSHALL STOOD AT THE EDGE OF THE SALLY'S BAR and Grill parking lot. A team of dogs had been borrowed from the FBI team which was searching for Sam Marino.

The dogs and the searchers fanned out through the parking lot after the instructions had been given. Sally stood beside Trevor, looking concerned.

"I told you he isn't here," she said. "He and Kendra left. We would have heard something. A scream, a gunshot."

"How loud was the music last night?" said Trevor.

"That's not important."

"Yes, it is."

"A gunshot is a gunshot. It's loud."

"Have you ever heard a gunshot before?"

"Ten years ago there was a shooting here," said Sally. "Back when Marino was in charge. Suppose that might be happening again? With him out of prison and the FBI moving through town?"

Trevor ignored her attempt to rile him up.

"You might not have recognized the gunshot," he said. "You might have thought it was a car backfiring, or maybe the gun was silenced. There are a lot of variables to consider."

"You think I don't know how to take care of my own property?"

Trevor turned to her. "Two people are missing. They're linked to this bar and to the prison escape of a major crime boss. Would you prefer to let him free on the town again?"

Sally looked back at the bar. Some people in the town, Trevor knew, would support a return to Marino rule. There was less money coming into the town. The price for a higher standard of life in Blind River was ignoring the occasional atrocity and denying any knowledge of it to the law enforcement who came asking. Trevor had always been shocked at how willing people were to look away.

"Yo, Detective!" one of the FBI K-9 agents shouted over. "We got something!"

Trevor smiled at Sally, who scoffed back at him. He walked to the edge of the parking lot where the FBI agent and his dog were standing. Beside him was another K-9 team. Both dogs were barking at the closed trunk of a car.

"Got him," said one of the Agents.

"Should we open it?" said Trevor.

"Go ahead and try."

Trevor took a deep breath and stepped up to the trunk. He tried opening it, but it was locked. "Can we get a lock-smith out here?"

"I'll get one of the FBI guys," said the Agent.

Trevor stepped back from the car. The dogs continued barking at it as though they knew exactly what was inside.

Trevor glanced at Sally, standing by the entrance to her bar and looking more worried than before.

The question wasn't what was in the trunk. It was who.

CHAPTER 48

NATASHA LEANED BACK AS JOE HAGERTY AND MATT OBERMAN stepped into the jail and walked to Bobby Randall's cell. The two officers stood at the bars, staring at the man suspected of murdering their loved ones.

Natasha smiled, hoping she was about to see something for the ages, something that would fit perfectly into her best-selling book. She was considering the title The Tragedy of Blind River: The Crumbling Town One Reporter Stood Up For. She leaned forward, not wanting to miss anything.

Ken Hagerty leaned back from the bars and stopped the endless tirade of insults and threats to which he'd been subjecting Bobby to. Instead, his eyes passed over his brother and the other officer.

"So, this is the man who killed my sister," said Matt.

"I didn't do it!" shouted Bobby Randall. His lawyer had been there earlier, but the lawyer had only told him not to say anything else without him present. Bobby had asked that he be transferred to another jail and that his innocence be noted. The lawyer had said he would do what he could, but couldn't promise anything.

"Why is the FBI talking to you if you haven't done anything?" said Joe. "You know, Officer Oberman and I have offered to watch the jail for the next few hours. The other officers were a little reluctant, but they came around." He grinned. "Until then, we can do whatever we want."

"What are you talking about?" There was a nervous stutter in Bobby's voice that hadn't been there before.

Natasha stood and walked closer to the bars.

"Ken," said Joe Hagerty, turning back to his brother and ignoring Natasha. "What would you do if you could get your hands on the man who killed your daughter?"

"I'd rip him limb from limb," said Ken, his hands grasping the bars of his cell. "I'd smash his head against the wall until his brain was dripping down the stone. I'd beat him until he could never hurt anyone ever again."

Bobby sunk farther into his cell. The cops laughed. For a moment Natasha thought they would stop there.

Joe took a key from his belt, glancing toward the door which led into the main station, and unlocked Ken's cell.

Ken frowned at the two officers as he stepped out of the cell.

Joe walked over to Bobby's cell and put the key into the lock.

"What the hell are you doing?" screamed Bobby, receding to the back of the cell. "Help!"

Natasha's heart pounded with excitement. They seemed to have forgotten she was there. She had a front-row seat. Bobby continued to scream, but the soundproof walls of the jail held firm.

The door to Bobby's cell slid open as he continued to scream. Ken gave a questioning glance to the officers, like a child asking his parents for permission. They both nodded and stepped back.

Ken smiled and stepped into the cell with the man he thought was his daughter's murderer, cracking his knuckles. He lunged, grabbed Bobby Randall, and threw him to the floor. Bobby's screams reached a new decibel. Ken straddled Bobby and began feeding him one punch after another. Teeth and blood flew into the air along with Bobby's screams and desperate protests. Blood coated Ken's fists, but he didn't slow. Matt turned away and took a few deep breaths.

"Stop!" Bobby screamed. "Please! I never touched her."

Matt glanced at Natasha, then looked away. They must have decided that her seeing the assault and murder in front of them was a necessary price. This was justice.

Natasha leaned through the cell bars, trying to improve her view of the blood covering the floor of the cell. Ken had lost all semblance of control, adrenaline, anger and animalistic rage taking over.

Unlike the others, however, Natasha knew Bobby was innocent. She knew that his cries were genuine, that he'd never touched the girls and didn't have the slightest idea what had happened to them. She also knew that she wasn't going to stop what was happening in front of her. She'd never seen a murder before, and it was better than she could ever have dreamed.

She'd been told in depth about the murders of the girls from the murderer's own lips, but there was something about seeing it with her own eyes she would never forget.

CHAPTER 49

TREVOR STEPPED BACK AS THE FBI AGENT UNLOCKED THE trunk and it popped open. A disgusting scent hit them like a tidal wave.

"What the hell is that?" said Sally, covering her nose.

"That's a dead body," said Trevor, plugging his nose. "Bowels emptied themselves. Is it Williams or Matheson?"

One of the FBI agents wearing rubber gloves stepped forward and examined the body. His calmness bothered Trevor more than it should.

"Male," said the Agent. "Prison ID on his belt. Nate Williams. Dead more than twelve hours, I'd guess."

"Shit," said Sally, taking a step back. The smell finally got to her. She ran to the ditch and lost her breakfast.

Trevor nodded and walked away, taking out his phone. He dialed Frankie's number.

"What is it, Trevor?" said Frankie, answering on the first ring.

"We've got Nate Williams."

"Good. Where was he?"

"Stuffed into a trunk outside Sally's Bar and Grill. Dead."

"God damn it. Is it the same killer?"

"I don't know. There's something else."

"What?" Frankie had the same calmness the other FBI agents had. Trevor wondered if they taught it at the academy.

"He was last seen with Kendra Matheson. We can't find her either."

"Shit."

"Yeah."

"Put out an APB on her."

"Do you think it's the killer?"

"We need to assume that," said Frankie.

"So it's not Bobby Randall?"

"He's certainly got a damn good alibi."

"Yeah."

"Get the body to Dr. Novak. Shut down the scene. Anything you find might point us to the killer. You're in charge."

Trevor glanced back at the FBI agents around the car. "Okay," he said. "I'll take care of things here."

CHAPTER 50

FRANKIE HUNG UP HER PHONE AND LOOKED BACK AT THE O'Connells' house. She'd been on her way out when Trevor called.

The O'Connells' had been delighted to hear that their daughter was alive based on Dr. Novak's discovery that the blood type didn't match. Unfortunately, however, they'd been unable to give Frankie any new information. She'd been hoping that Miranda had contacted them, but she'd had no such luck.

Curtis wasn't answering his phone, and so she called the hospital and learned that Gordon Mackley had passed.

She had met the man just once a few nights earlier, but she'd heard enough about his legacy to understand what a tragedy it was for Blind River.

There would be a funeral with a grand attendance, and his coffin would be expensive and well made. Chief Tucker would give a eulogy, and the town would mourn. A local hero, a pillar of the community, and a key part in expelling Marino, was gone from the world.

She didn't have long to think about the ramifications of Gordon's death when her phone rang again.

"Hello?" she answered.

"Hey," said Chief Tucker.

There was an uneasiness in his voice Frankie didn't like. "What happened?"

"We've had an issue at the station," said Tucker.

"What happened?"

"Two of our officers made a mistake, and there will be consequences."

"What happened?"

"Oberman and Hagerty went into the prison, and something happened."

Frankie took a deep breath. "Tell me what happened, right now, in as few words as possible. I don't have time to talk."

"Ken Hagerty beat Bobby Randall to death."

Frankie took another breath, clenching and unclenching her fists. She was barely holding her anger in check. "Are you fucking kidding me?"

"We made a mistake," said Tucker sheepishly.

"Tell me what happened. Everything."

Tucker recounted what had happened in the jail in extreme detail, frequently pushing the blame off himself and onto other members of the police force.

When he'd finished, Frankie said, "Where are Oberman and Hagerty now?"

"They're in the jail, as prisoners. Ken is back in his own cell. A doctor tried to save Bobby Randall, but there was nothing she could do. The body's in the morgue with Dr. Novak. Not that she'll find anything new. We have the security footage. We know exactly what happened." He paused. "I suppose you've heard about Gordon Mackley."

"And I suppose you've heard about Trevor's discovery."

"Yes."

They were both silent for a few moments. Despite their combined experience, neither had ever been confronted with so many concurrent major issues.

Frankie tried to think it through.

The town was crawling with FBI agents, Sam Marino was loose, two cops had gone rogue and murdered a probably innocent murder suspect, a serial killer was probably still free somewhere, and the former chief had died.

Frankie came to the silent conclusion that she needed to write everything down.

Frankie let out a deep sigh. "Leave Oberman and Hagerty in the jail, but tell them about Trevor's discovery. We'll deal with them later. They'll be charged as accomplices to Ken Hagerty's first-degree murder. I'll pick up Curtis from the hospital and meet you there. We'll try to figure out our next move."

Tucker agreed, and they ended the call. Frankie got to her car and drove away from the O'Connells' house. She wondered what had become of Miranda O'Connell if she was still alive somewhere, and also who the fourth body belonged to.

For now, those questions could wait.

She pulled into the hospital and parked in the waiting zone, making sure her FBI credentials were hanging from the mirror.

She walked inside. Hospitals always made her feel

uncomfortable, as though she was seeing too deeply into the human experience.

She entered Gordon Mackley's room. The bed was empty. Apparently, the body had been moved to the morgue.

At the bottom of the bed were Monica and Curtis, sitting in silence. They looked up when Frankie entered.

"I'm sorry for your loss," she said softly, "but we need to go."

Curtis's voice was monotone, devoid of emotion. "My father's dead. Can't you take care of it?"

"Bobby Randall and Nate Williams are both dead. Marino is still out there, and Kendra Matheson has been taken."

Curtis's gaze focused. He became serious and concerned, the look of a man who had never wanted to do anything in life except help people. "What happened?" he said.

Frankie brought him up to speed as quickly as she could. When she finished, Curtis was already standing and walking out the door. The moment she'd mentioned Bobby he'd jumped to his feet.

"Monica," he said, "are you coming?"

"No," said Monica, staring blankly forward. "I'll stay here and deal with the stuff for Dad."

"Are you sure?"

Monica nodded, then turned to them. "Find Kendra and that asshole Marino. I'll be here."

Curtis considered pushing the point, then decided against it. "Okay," he said.

They left the hospital without another word and drove to the police station. Chief Tucker and Trevor were waiting for them in the war room.

"I want to speak with Oberman and Hagerty," said Curtis as they took their seats.

Chief Tucker pinched the bridge of his nose. "Are we certain Bobby Randall isn't the murderer? This other kidnapping could be a fluke."

Frankie shook her head. "The chances of another kidnapper in a town this small are so low as to be non-existent."

"What about Marino? Could he be the new killer?"

"It's possible, but it wouldn't make any sense. Why would he attack someone when he first got out of prison? He's home free, why leave a trail of breadcrumbs?"

"But it's possible?" said Tucker.

Frankie shrugged. "Anything's possible, but it doesn't make sense. Marino is trying to stay out of prison and rebuild his connections. A lot of the citizens in this town aren't convinced their lives are any better than when he was in charge. He's probably hiding out with one of them right now."

Tucker nodded, although he seemed like he wanted to defend his town.

Curtis leaned forward, between Frankie and Tucker. "Why don't Frankie and I go speak with the officers? Then I'll speak with Robert Randall about how his son was brutally murdered in a prison cell for a murder he didn't commit. Any objections?"

Chief Tucker and Trevor both seemed about to protest but decided otherwise.

Curtis nodded. He walked out of the office and toward the jail. Two FBI agents guarded the entrance. Curtis and Frankie presented their identification before being let inside. Ken

Hagerty was back in the first cell on the left, leaning against the wall, his expression blank. His hands and shirt were covered in blood.

Across from him was Natasha Nolowinski. Curtis tried not to imagine what Natasha would write when she was released. They still hadn't found Frankie's notepad and had no proof she'd taken it.

Natasha's expression as she watched him made Curtis uneasy. She had a smirk which normally meant she knew something he didn't.

They walked to the two back cells of the jail. On the left was the cell where the murder had taken place. Blood was smeared on the ground. It looked like an unenthusiastic janitor had come through with a wet mop and spread the blood around in an effort to clean it. Across from that grisly scene were the two officers.

Joe Hagerty sat on a bench in the corner, staring at the back wall of the cell, motionless, his knees pulled to his chest. Matt Oberman was pacing back and forth, wringing his hands in front of his body and muttering to himself. Based on the words Curtis was able to make out, he was trying to convince himself he'd done the right thing.

Curtis had to shout at Matt a few times to get his attention. He paused and looked up at Curtis with a curious expression.

"What were you thinking?" said Curtis, standing a few feet in front of the cell. Frankie stood behind him.

Oberman turned. When he spoke, his voice was faint. "I was trying to avenge my sister," he said. "He killed her and threw her body in a river."

"No, he didn't."

"Yes, he did!" Matt lunged at the bars, screaming. "He fucking killed her."

Curtis took a step back in surprise at the instability that had so quickly come over Matt. Curtis looked him in the eyes.

"Whatever happened to the oath you swore when you became a police officer?" he said. "Is this how the justice system in this country is supposed to work? Like some savage revenge scheme? Maybe you think we should just murder everyone who's ever been suspected of anything?"

A calmness came over Matt. He shook his head and smiled incredulously. "You don't know what it's like," he said. "You try knowing that someone you love has probably been raped, murdered and subjected to torture you can't even imagine. If that day ever comes, I'll hand you a gun and give you the bullets. I'll help you point that gun at the suspect. At that moment, you'll understand why I did what I did. And you'll pull the trigger, because that's what family is."

Curtis let out a deep sigh. "That isn't how a civilized society works. The justice system would have found if he was guilty, and if he was, we would have done the right thing and imprisoned him."

Matt shook his head and stepped back from the bars. "If you ever find yourself in that position, with a loaded gun pointing at the person who ripped away a loved one, remember this conversation. On that day, I'll accept your apology."

Matt walked to the back of the cell and fell onto the bench. He crossed his arms and looked away, making it clear the conversation was over.

"Hey, Hagerty!" said Curtis, gesturing to the curled-up

mess of a man in the corner of the cell. "What do you think of this?"

"You won't get a response," said Natasha.

Curtis and Frankie turned to see Natasha leaning through the bars of her cell and looking at them.

"I've been trying all day," she said. "He and Ken aren't responding at all. Makes it hard to get a quote."

Frankie walked to the front of Natasha's cell. "Don't you have any shame?"

Natasha smirked. "Shame is a five-letter word that means lack of ambition."

Frankie turned away from her. "Curtis, let's get out of here."

Curtis followed Frankie, glancing back at Natasha for a moment, still getting that feeling she knew something they didn't. He shrugged it off and walked to the car with Frankie.

Trevor had left to continue his search for Kendra Matheson. FBI agents were looking for Marino. Curtis and Frankie were on their way to notify Robert Randall about his son, then they would continue looking for the true killer.

Somewhere in the back of Curtis's mind was the knowledge that his father was dead, that Monica was probably picking out a casket for him at that moment. Once this was finished, for better or worse, he would think of himself.

For now, he had to push aside his own wishes for the greater good.

He'd done it before.

CHAPTER 51

ROBERT RANDALL RUBBED THE CLOTH AGAINST THE COUNTER, trying to get out an annoying stain. He looked up at the empty bar and wondered where Bobby was. His son was supposed to be in before ten. He was half an hour late.

He sighed and returned to his cleaning. He heard the door open and said, without looking, "Sorry, we're closed until noon."

"I'm not allowed to come in and visit an old friend?"

Robert wrung out the cloth in the sink before looking up at Sam Marino.

The escaped prisoner stood on the other side of the bar with the same bewildering confidence he'd always had. Marino was wearing a basic white t-shirt, dirty jeans, and a ratty Buffalo Bills cap.

"Sam," said Robert blankly.

Marino spread his arms as though looking for a hug. Robert put his hands on top of the bar and stared at him.

"That's no way to greet an old friend," said Marino.

"What are you doing here, Sam?"

"You didn't hear I'd escaped?"

"I thought you'd be out of town. FBI agents are everywhere."

"This is my town, Robert," said Marino with a smile. "I want your help to get it back."

Robert leaned forward. "Why would I help you with anything?"

Marino laughed. "They never even thought to suspect you, did they? The friendly, joyous, Santa Claus-looking bartender could never hurt anyone. But I've seen what you are capable of, Robert. What? You forget you worked for me? You forget working as my muscle and that you requested to kill those kids?"

Robert moved his hand behind the bar. His fingers grazed the barrel of a shotgun hanging there.

"The moment I heard about the girls," said Marino, "I knew it was you. It couldn't have been anyone else."

Robert's hand rested on the shotgun's barrel. "What do you want?"

Sam shrugged as though it was obvious. "I want you to become my right-hand man while I rebuild my empire."

"Get out of my bar. I will shoot you, and I will be within my rights. They might even give me a medal."

"And what if they come looking for the Matheson girl? You snatched her from a bar last night while she was drunk? Seems lazy."

Robert shrugged. "Get out, or I'm calling the cops."

Marino glanced out the window and frowned. "Did you call them already?"

"No, what are you talking about?"

Robert followed where Marino was looking. Curtis

Mackley and Frankie Lassiter parked in front of the bar. They had no backup and no sirens, nor any sense of urgency as they climbed out.

"I don't need to tell you that I'm not here," said Marino, slipping around the back of the bar and into the kitchen.

CHAPTER 52

CURTIS READIED HIMSELF TO STEP INTO THE BAR AND TELL Robert that his son had been murdered in cold blood in the middle of the police station. He checked his watch five times as they walked to the door. The time never changed.

They stepped into the bar. It was empty save for Robert Randall rubbing a spot out of the counter he seemingly couldn't get. He looked up when he saw Curtis, and his face broke out into a broad grin.

"Curtis!" he bellowed. "How nice to see you!"

The agents stepped up to the bar.

"Robert, we need to talk," said Curtis, stepping up to the bar. "We fucked up, to be completely honest."

"What happened?" said Robert. "I'm sure it's not that bad."

Curtis took a deep breath. "Bobby's dead."

Robert didn't reply for a moment. "What?"

Curtis took another breath and told him what had happened. Robert's face lost all emotion, becoming an unreadable canvas.

When Curtis was finished, he said, "Which cops?"

"Hagerty and Oberman. I'm so sorry."

Robert lowered his head. "Marino's in the kitchen."

"What?" Frankie jerked her head around.

"Sam Marino is in the kitchen."

There was the sound of running through the kitchen and a door slamming.

"Frankie! Call it in!" Curtis took off at a sprint, pulling his gun from its holster and running behind the bar.

He ran through the kitchen, then out the back door. There, on the edge of the forest behind the bar, was Marino, his form distinct, but shrinking into the distance and the cover that the trees provided.

"Sam Marino! Freeze! FBI!"

Marino disappeared between the trees.

Curtis grinned. This was the chance he'd been waiting for since that night Josh disappeared. The missing girls, the murders at the station, his deceased father, none of it mattered anymore. He sped up and ran toward the forest, closing the distance between himself and Marino.

CHAPTER 53

FRANKIE TURNED AWAY FROM ROBERT RANDALL AND GRABBED her radio.

"Dispatch, come in. This is FBI Special Agent Frankie Lassiter. I need backup at—"

Frankie turned and looked directly into the barrel of a shotgun.

"At where?" said the radio.

Robert had rounded the counter with such quiet steps that Frankie hadn't sensed him approaching. It seemed impossible that a man of his girth could be so quiet.

"Robert," said Frankie, raising her hands into the air. The radio continued to make noise, asking for information. "What are you doing?"

"Drop that radio and slide it over to me," said Robert. "Slowly. If you go for your gun, I'll blow your brains out."

There was a vacantness in Robert's eyes Frankie had only ever seen in serial killers, and at that moment, she saw how they'd gotten everything wrong, how they had been so close to the correct answer.

She bent over and slid the radio across the floor. As she stood, she looked out the front window of the bar, hoping that some passing cop would see their car and figure out where they were.

Robert stomped on the radio, crushing it under his foot. "Give me your gun."

Frankie nodded and took her gun from its holster. She remained calm and looked for any opening, but Robert never took his eyes off her, his finger twitching on the trigger of the shotgun. She slid the gun along the floor. Robert kicked it away, into the corner.

"Why do this?" she said.

Robert didn't take his eyes off her for a moment. "Sam Marino showed me the joy of killing a long time ago," he said. "This is something I'm good at, something I'm passionate about. I'd forgotten the feeling when Ashley Hagerty fell into my lap. Killing is like riding a bicycle. You never forget."

"You're murdering people."

Robert shrugged. "To each their own. Now give me your car keys."

Frankie slid them along the floor. There was no opening as he bent over and grabbed the keys, the gun still leveled at her head.

"Get up and walk to the stairs."

"Where?"

Robert pointed with his free hand at the door to his right, which had a sign saying, "Employees only."

Frankie stood and walked to the door, looking for the opening she was getting certain would never come. She opened the door, which led to a staircase and a cellar. She took the steps slowly, Robert following a few steps behind.

"Turn right," said Robert when she reached the bottom of the stairs. "Open the freezer."

Freezer, thought Frankie, remembering that Dr. Novak had said the victims had indications of frostbite.

Frankie walked to the large steel door and unlocked it. She grabbed the handle and pulled the thick door open. It was at least a foot thick, more than enough to muffle any sounds. A blast of freezing air hit her in the face, and an involuntary shiver racked her body.

"Who's there?" came a voice from inside.

"Kendra?" said Frankie, looking into the dark freezer, lit only by the light of the cellar behind them.

"Agent Lassiter?" said Kendra.

"Get in," said Robert, "or I'll shoot both of you."

Frankie hesitated and got the shotgun shoved into her back.

She stumbled inside the freezer, slipping on the icy floor and catching herself against the wall. She spun back toward the door just as it slammed shut. The sound of the lock sliding into place echoed through the freezer.

"Shit," said Frankie, moving across the ten by ten freezer, now dark except for the dim light coming through the small window. She moved her hands over the door, looking for the handle.

"It's—it's not there," said Kendra from the corner of the freezer, a shiver in her voice. "No door handle, no light. No food. He moved it all some--somewhere else."

Frankie turned around and looked around the freezer. There were shelves around the edges built into the freezer, but there was no food on the shelves. The entire freezer was coated in a thin layer of ice and snow.

Kendra sat against the wall, her arms wrapped around herself. She was wearing a thick parka and gloves, which looked as though they'd been supplied by Robert. Perhaps he wanted to kill his victims himself. He wouldn't let the cold do it for him. Even with the parka, she was shivering.

Frankie paced back and forth once, pulling her jacket around herself. "Fuck! We should have seen it. We never even considered Robert."

"No one did," said Kendra. A shiver wracked her entire body. "No one did."

Frankie sighed, turning and looking out the window of the freezer, wondering whether they would ever get out. "I should have seen it."

CHAPTER 54

Curtis sprinted through the forest as it became denser, pushing branches away and trying not to trip. He couldn't see Marino but could hear the panting of a winded man less than a dozen feet in front of him.

Curtis had his gun ready. There was light gathering in front of him.

The branches continued to snap back, cutting his skin and ripping his clothes. All he could think was how close he was to getting Marino, to having him alone. He could finally learn what happened to Josh. He could finally know.

He broke through the underbrush and into a clearing, the sun coming like an onslaught against his eyes. He put his arm over his head to block out the sunlight and only saw Marino sprinting directly at him at the last second.

Curtis got his hands in front of his face to block the blow from the shorter but thicker Marino and managed to block it. His gun went flying from his hands, bouncing across the ground and settling in a patch of grass.

Both men lunged for the gun.

Curtis got there first. As he bent over to get it, Marino tackled him from behind, sending him spinning and falling to the ground.

Marino got on top of him, straddling Curtis's chest and pinning Curtis's arms. Curtis tried to move, but was unable to get any leverage.

Marino grinned through his red, sweat-covered face. "Here we are, Curtis," he said. "I have you at my mercy. I'll bet you wish you hadn't turned me in to the feds now. Maybe if you hadn't, I would let you leave here alive."

"If I die," said Curtis, "I'm taking you with me."

Marino just laughed and looked around. When he saw the gun sitting ten feet away, he sighed. "Suppose I won't be able to get that without letting you up. Guess I'll have to do this the old-fashioned way." He grinned. "You really thought I didn't know it was you? I always knew it was you, you little piece of shit."

"I didn't buy your lies and your nice guy act for a second," said Curtis.

"Whatever you say." Marino put his hands around Curtis's throat, choking him and cutting off his airway. "I'm going to enjoy this."

Curtis tried to reply, but he was already losing air, and his words came out as strained gasps. He shook his arms, trying to get out from beneath Marino as thumbs dug into his windpipe. He flailed his legs against Marino's back, trying to get him to loosen his grip.

Marino was breathing heavily and grunted.

The blue of the sky above Curtis grew hazy. The world began going out of focus. He gasped for the air that couldn't get to his lungs.

He lunged forward in a last moment effort as though he was doing a sit-up and at that moment managed to get his chin against his chest, allowing him to gasp for air.

Marino kept fighting, far from defeated, and Curtis knew that the rush of air that flowed into his lungs would be useless if he couldn't get out from under Marino. With the rush of air that went into his brain, he did the only thing that seemed to have any chance of working.

He lunged forward and bit down as hard as he could on the side of Marino's hand, his teeth sinking into the right thumb.

Marino screamed as Curtis's teeth sunk through flesh and muscle down to the bone. Curtis could taste blood in his mouth. He didn't let go as Marino yanked back his hand, trying desperately to pry it loose of Curtis's jaws.

Marino looked angrier than anyone Curtis had ever seen. The former crime boss raised his free hand into the air, ready to punch the side of Curtis's face and free his hand. It didn't seem to occur to him that if Curtis didn't let go, he'd effectively be ripping his thumb off.

Curtis took the chance of Marino being off-balance to use his freed arm to grab him and force him off.

Marino went sprawling across the grass, blood flowing from his hand. The skin from his thumb was hanging from Curtis's teeth as he stood.

He took a few deep breaths and checked his throat for damage. He tore the piece of flesh from his teeth. The taste of Marino's blood was still fresh. He spat onto the ground, but it did little to get rid of the taste.

Marino spun to a standing position and grabbed his hand

in an attempt to stop the bleeding. He looked down and smiled.

Curtis's gun was sitting at his feet. His movements were slowed from his blood loss, but he was still able to grab the gun off the ground with his free hand while he pushed his wound into his shirt. The shirt quickly became a deep red.

Curtis was too far away. He raised his hands in surrender as Marino leveled the gun at him. Marino wobbled, looking lightheaded from blood loss.

At that moment, Curtis took a gamble he knew was all or nothing. He sprinted at Marino with all his energy.

The sound of the gunshot echoed through the forest, but Curtis didn't think he'd been hit. He tackled Marino, shoulder first, as hard as he could. Marino went sliding along the ground and into a tree at the edge of the clearing, groaning loudly.

The gun slid along the ground five feet away from him. Curtis walked over to the gun and picked it up. He was panting heavily, his entire body still screaming from a lack of oxygen, his head pounding, his clothes soaked in sweat from the scorching sun above them.

Curtis turned and raised the gun, pointing it at Marino's head.

Marino had managed to turn around and was sitting against a tree, his shirt wrapped around his injured hand. Blood still flowed onto his shirt.

"Are you going to shoot me?" said Marino, strangely calm. "You ruined my entire life. You destroyed everything I spent my entire life building. Why not finish it off?"

As much as Curtis wanted to put a bullet through Marino's head, he took a deep breath and returned his gun to the holster. He took out his cell phone.

"You know, Josh was weak, too," said Marino, a chuckle passing through his lips. "Right up until the end."

Curtis spun back to him, his phone in one hand and the other going to his gun. "What did you say?"

Marino smirked. "Josh was weak. He was one of the best of the people in my network, but he wanted too much. He thought he would take over from me, that he could lead better than I could. So I cracked his skull with a baseball bat in front of everyone. I let him bleed out on the floor as an example. We buried Josh's body so deep in the forest no one would ever find it, where the scavenging animals would eat it until there was nothing left but bones, and the bones would disintegrate and return to nature. Now tell me, Curtis, are you still going to leave me alive, knowing what I did to your brother?"

Curtis stood there for a few moments, letting the new information seep in. He knew Marino was baiting him, trying to do anything not to return to his cell. Somehow, Curtis knew it was the truth. He had always suspected Marino had been connected to Josh's disappearance, and that Josh's own actions had been at least partly responsible.

He didn't feel the need for vengeance that Matt Oberman had insisted he would feel. He felt something different.

At that moment, Curtis understood how the O'Connells could have misidentified their daughter's body in the morgue, how the relief had washed over the other parents when they identified their own offspring. It was the weight of uncertainty being lifted off their shoulders. For the first time in decades, Curtis felt at peace.

"No," he said to Marino. "You don't deserve a quick death." He took out his phone and dialed Frankie's number.

Marino glared at him, the light going out of his eyes more and more as the blood from his hand soaked the shirt.

Curtis frowned as the call rang and no one answered. As Frankie's voicemail message played, he realized that he had never heard the message before. Frankie always answered her phone. She believed a federal agent should always be reachable.

Curtis ended the call without leaving a message and called Trevor. Trevor answered on the third ring. "Curtis," he said, "what the hell happened?"

"I have Marino. He was at Randall's Pub. What are you talking about?"

"Frankie sent out a communication that got cut off about Marino," said Trevor. "We haven't been able to reach her. I'm heading over to Randall's Tavern now. Call Tucker and tell him where Marino is. Meet me at the tavern."

Before Curtis could answer, the call ended. Curtis turned and was about to call Tucker when he thought of something he couldn't believe hadn't occurred to him earlier.

He turned back to Marino. "Why were you at the tavern?"

Marino laughed. "Because I needed some muscle, and Robert Randall is one of the best in the business."

"What are you talking about?" Curtis tried to process what he was saying.

Marino laughed again. "You should have seen him in his prime. He was an insane motherfucker. I killed people because I had a reason, but Robert didn't need any of that. It was like a drug to him. He once told me that if he didn't feel the life leave someone on a regular basis, he started getting cold shakes and headaches. If there was a support group for serial killers, he would have been there in a second."

The pieces started to fall together in Curtis's head too perfectly to ignore. He could see it. Robert Randall living a law-abiding life while the rest of the criminals he'd associated with languished behind bars. He'd lived with his addiction, ignoring the urges that came to him. Then he'd learned that Bobby was sneaking alcohol to the high schoolers, and all of a sudden he had a new outlet. He knew about the pond in the forest because Curtis had told him about it twenty years earlier when Robert had been sneaking alcohol to him and Jeff.

He must have gone to an adjacent town to get that first kill, that unidentified body in the river, to get the feeling back, then had come back to Blind River, watching the girls Bobby was sneaking booze to. When he saw his chances, he took them, and that was how he had killed the three local girls.

In his mind's eye, he saw Frankie standing in the middle of the bar without that knowledge, moments after they had told a serial killer that his son had been murdered by the cops.

Curtis dialed the police station as quickly as he could, a cold sweat coming over him.

Behind him, Marino laughed.

CHAPTER 55

ROBERT RANDALL PARKED AND CLIMBED OUT OF HIS CAR. HE checked that the handgun was securely attached to his waist and wasn't immediately visible.

A few police officers nodded to him as he walked toward the station. He nodded back, remaining calm. He would have preferred to bring the shotgun, but there was no way he would get into the building.

He stepped inside and the receptionist gave him a sympathetic look. She covered the mouthpiece to the phone she was talking on. "The chief is in the jail dealing with some things," she said. "If you go to his office, he'll be there in a moment. I'm so sorry for what happened."

Robert nodded, trying to look as stoic and sad as he could. He felt nothing for his son and never had. Everything he'd ever done for Bobby was done with the intention of keeping up appearances, of appearing to be the joyous and loving fat guy everyone in town loved. He wanted to seem like a loving father.

He was about to do what any loving father would do.

He walked through the station, getting sympathetic nods and averted glances. Not a single person, FBI nor police, checked him for weapons. This was what his carefully cultivated personality had earned him, the right to not be suspected. He walked to the door of the jail. The FBI agent standing there put up a hand.

"I'm sorry, Mr. Randall," he said. "You can't go in."

"My son died in there." His voice was intentionally desperate and pleading.

"I'm sorry. You can't."

Robert sighed and nodded. He took the gun from his waistband and shoved it into the agent's ribs. The agent's eyes opened wide, but he said nothing. Robert glanced over his shoulder at the station. No one had reacted.

"Open the door," said Robert.

The agent grabbed the keycard from his waist, his fingers fumbling with the card. The door clicked open.

"Come with me," said Robert, walking the agent backward into the jail.

Inside, Chief Tucker was standing outside the second cell on the right, leaning through the bars. He was lecturing someone and didn't look up when Robert entered. Robert locked the door of the jail. The loud click made the occupants of the cells look up.

Robert smiled at Natasha in the cell to his right. She smiled back. He had missed her. She was one of the only people who understood him.

"Robert?" said Chief Tucker, stepping back from the bars and looking up. "Can you wait in my office? You can't be in here."

Robert didn't reply. He shoved the agent forward,

revealing the gun. "You're responsible for my son's death."

He glanced to the left, seeing Ken Hagerty. He kept the gun trained on Chief Tucker, who had moved into a shooters stance, his left foot forward and his hand on his gun.

"Robert, put down the gun," said Tucker. "I'll be forced to shoot you. I understand you're upset, but I won't have any more bloodshed here. Wait outside."

"He killed my son," said Robert, gesturing at Ken.

Ken didn't reply. He almost seemed accepting of his fate.

"Robert, I'm warning you," said Tucker.

"Chief, can I ask you something?"

Chief Tucker frowned.

"Have you ever shot someone?"

"What?"

Robert rolled his neck to get out a kink. "I asked if you'd ever shot someone. You became chief after Marino and his cronies were in prison. You've never lived or been the chief in a town filled with crime, a town where people die every day. Have you ever pulled out your gun and shot somebody?"

Tucker didn't respond, his hand still on the gun. The FBI agent Robert had taken hostage was on the ground a few feet away, looking up at him.

"That's a shame," said Robert, "because I have."

He fired once at Chief Tucker. The chief took the bullet in the center of his forehead and pitched backward. His gun was still holstered.

The agent began to scream for help. Robert put one between his eyes as well.

"What the fuck?" screamed Ken Hagerty, scrambling to the back of his cell.

"Wait your turn," said Robert calmly.

There were sounds of commotion coming from inside the station. Apparently, the soundproof walls didn't work with gunshots.

Robert bent over and grabbed the ring of keys and the gun from Chief Tucker's waist. He looked to his right, at Matt Oberman and Joe Hagerty. They were the two officers who'd been responsible for the death of his son. He smiled at them with his most joyous and happy smile. Neither of the officers said a word, as though hoping to blend into the walls.

Robert stood and looked back, seeing the partially cleaned blood on the floor of the cell where his son had been. For a moment, he felt what most people would call empathy. Then it was gone, and he was just a man with a task. This was what a father did when his child was murdered. There was nothing he could do about it.

The door to the jail began rattling as officers responded to the gunshots. Someone shouted for keys.

Robert walked back to Natasha's cell. Robert unlocked the cell. She stood and walked up to him.

"It's good to see you again," said Robert.

"I missed you." Natasha went up on her tiptoes and kissed him.

He smiled back at her, holding out the gun he'd taken from Chief Tucker. "Don't let anyone in, but don't shoot unless you have to."

Natasha took the gun and slid it into the back of her pants. "I have a better idea," she said. She turned and walked to the door, from the other side of which came the jingle of keys.

"Help!" Natasha screamed through the door, "Don't come in! He's going to kill me!"

Robert smiled as the jingling ceased, replaced with frantic whispering. He'd known Natasha was someone who could understand him from the first time he'd met her, although their relationship hadn't flourished until he'd started killing again.

As soon as he'd seen her stories in the Blind River Observer and realized that she understood, he had propositioned her with an offer. She could write the story about the case once it was all over, and in return he would feed her information that only the cops and the killer would have. There had always been a chance she would turn him in, but he'd never worried.

It had also caused the unexpected advantage of the cops thinking one of their own were giving information to the paper, causing a sense of distrust which Robert believed had helped his killing spree.

From that point on, he and Natasha's relationship had only grown, until he had come to think that she was the only woman he'd ever met who understood him, more than his wife, more than his mother. They had a connection he hadn't believed possible. She had listened while he proudly recounted killing the girls, of kidnapping them and keeping them in the freezer beneath his bar, of strangling them, of throwing them into the river where they would sink to the bottom and their bodies would disappear, never to be found.

Of course, they had been found. He'd never imagined that Curtis Mackley, one of the only people who knew about the pond and its secret, would come back to investigate.

"Help!" Natasha cried again. "He's going to kill everyone!"

She turned back and gave Robert a playful smile.

"What the fuck is wrong with you people?" shouted Ken Hagerty from his cell.

"Wait your turn," said Robert. "I've got to do this in order. Those two first."

He walked to the cell where Oberman and Hagerty were being kept, both of whom were wide-eyed and terrified. They'd been stripped of their weapons.

The shot he put into each of their heads didn't meet any resistance. They slumped against the wall beside each other, still seated on the bench. It had been more of an execution than a killing.

Robert didn't mind.

"That's amazing," said Natasha. "How are you so accurate?"

"Staying calm and lots of practice, sweetie. Just one more, then we can get out of here."

"Get out of here?"

"I have a plan," he said. "Just one more thing to do, isn't there, Ken?"

Ken had pushed himself against the wall of the cell, his eyes wide in the same abject terror Robert had seen from his other victims.

"Please," said Ken, "I thought he killed my daughter. My Ashley. I made a mistake. I'm sorry."

"I understand."

Ken looked up at him. "You do?"

"Yes, I do." Robert smiled. "If I thought someone had killed my son, I would do everything I could to make sure he was buried so deep underground that he never saw a moment of sunlight. I understand completely."

With that, he fired the gun's fifth bullet, followed by the

sixth. One hit Ken in the chest and the other in the cheek. He fell to the ground, grabbing his chest frantically, his movements slowing as he lost strength. Robert looked at the empty gun in his hand and threw it onto the floor. It stopped a few feet away from Ken, who looked at it for a moment through his strained breaths.

"Pass me the gun," said Robert. Natasha gave him Chief Tucker's gun. Robert checked the magazine. Four bullets.

Chief Tucker needed to check his bullets more often. The maintenance on the gun was so poor Robert worried it would backfire.

He grabbed Natasha, pulling her toward him and kissing her as passionately as he could. After a moment, she returned the kiss. They held each other there for a moment, his beard brushing against her perfect skin and her hair falling into his eyes. They held each other in an embrace of true love in the middle of a jail filled with death.

After a few moments, Robert spun Natasha around so she was facing away and put the gun to her head. "This is how we're getting out of here," he said. "Make sure to look afraid."

Natasha nodded. Robert could feel her heartbeat against him. It excited him.

"Unlock the door," he said. Robert glanced behind him and saw the death and misery he'd caused. It made him feel warm inside.

Natasha unlocked the door, swinging it open to reveal the station. Police officers were gathered around, their guns aimed at the jail door. They all looked uneasy when they saw Natasha squirming and grabbing at Robert's arm, the gun pressed to her temple as he walked out. Her legs flailed against him, but he made no response.

"Help!" Natasha screamed.

"Anyone do anything," said Robert calmly, "And I blow her brains out."

None of the cops nor agents knew what to do. They looked helpless. Robert was able to walk around the edge of the station, his back to the wall, all the way to the door.

Natasha kept screaming and flailing, playing her role to perfection. They made it out to the parking lot without a single shot fired.

They walked backward to Robert's car. With his free hand, he took the keys from his pocket and unlocked it.

"Open the trunk," he said. The cops and agents were moving out of the police station and into the parking lot around them.

Natasha gave him an angry glare.

"Get into the trunk, or I will shoot you."

Natasha nodded, opened the trunk and climbed in. She would understand eventually.

Robert slammed the trunk, then walked to the driver's seat. He pulled out of the parking lot and onto the street as aggressively as he could, sending the message to the police that a few more casualties would mean nothing. He hit a speed bump and heard Natasha smash against the top of the trunk.

He could hear her muffled curses, but he kept driving.

They had to get out of Blind River as fast as possible.

It was the only way they could have a life together.

CHAPTER 56

CURTIS MADE IT BACK TO THE PUB JUST AS TREVOR PULLED INTO the parking lot.

"Where is Frankie?" said Curtis as Trevor stepped out of the car.

"I don't know," said Trevor. "She was inside?"

"Yes!" Curtis could feel a cold sweat breaking out on the backs of his hands.

"Okay, lets--"

They were cut off as the radio inside Trevor's car started calling out, "All units report in! All units!"

Curtis nodded to the car and Trevor leaned inside. He listened for a few moments.

His face went white and scared. When he finished, he stepped out of the car with a blank expression, as though the world had lost all color.

"What happened?" said Curtis.

Trevor didn't respond. He didn't even seem aware of Curtis's existence.

Curtis grabbed his arm and spoke slowly. "What happened?"

Trevor focused on him. "Robert Randall attacked the station," he said. "Chief Tucker, Officers Hagerty and Oberman, Ken Hagerty, and one of the FBI agents are all dead. He took Nolowinski captive."

Curtis took a deep breath, assessing the new information.

"Trevor, I'm putting you in charge," he said. "Send a message to all available units to block off all exits from Blind River. Randall will be trying to get somewhere where he can start a new life. He'll want to find somewhere he can kill more people. Every moment we wait is a moment he could be leaving town. Tell the police, tell the news, tell Facebook, tell everyone you know. Ten thousand dollars paid by the FBI for any information leading to an arrest. Put it out now."

Curtis didn't know whether or not the FBI would pay, but it sounded realistic, and there wasn't time to check.

Trevor nodded frantically. "Okay, anything else?"

"No, do it now. Use my authority to make sure they follow through. I'm going to find Frankie."

Curtis turned and ran into the bar. He pulled out his gun and kept it at the ready. He walked through the quiet bar.

"Frankie!" he shouted.

He heard nothing. He cleared the kitchen, then came back to the main bar area. The basement was the only place he hadn't checked. He walked down the stairs, the steps creaking.

At the bottom, he swung his gun from side to side. His heart jumped when he saw movement to his right. He spun and saw it was the window of a freezer.

He took a few steps until he was certain he'd seen movement behind the small window. He unlocked and cranked open the door, light spilling into the freezer and onto the two people inside.

"Frankie, thank God!" said Curtis.

"Curtis?" Frankie lowered her hands and stood slowly, as though her limbs were frozen. She stumbled forward and hugged Curtis like he was a long-lost brother. He held her there in the cold air emanating from the freezer, looking over her shoulder at the hunched-over form in the corner. It took a few moments to recognize Kendra Matheson, wrapped in a heavy parka and in obvious need of medical attention.

"Come on," said Curtis, releasing himself from Frankie's grasp and walking into the freezer. He took Kendra's cold hand and helped her stand. Kendra was unable to speak and only barely able to nod, her movements stiff and inconsistent.

When they got out of the freezer, Kendra continued shivering despite the humid air.

"We need to get her to a hospital," said Frankie.

Curtis nodded. "Trevor's outside. Come on."

As they were walking up the stairs, going slow to accommodate the small steps Kendra was capable of, Frankie filled Curtis in on what had happened, recounting what Kendra had told her.

They exited the bar and stepped into the sun. Trevor was standing beside his car, talking frantically on the phone. He gave a rushed ending to his conversation and put his phone back in the car.

He ran to meet them, explaining that roadblocks were being set up at all exits from Blind River. He quickly agreed to take Kendra to the hospital. Trevor led Kendra to his car and put her in the passenger seat. He drove away and turned toward the hospital.

Frankie turned to Curtis. "Roadblocks? What happened?"

As they walked to Curtis's car, he explained what had happened, including Marino and the events at the station.

When he finished, Frankie took a few moments to answer, as though trying to figure out where to begin. "Is Marino still out there?"

Curtis climbed into the car and put the keys in the ignition. "I gave his coordinates to the team of FBI agents who were sent to find him. They'll deal with him."

Frankie nodded, buckling her seatbelt. "Chief Tucker's really dead?"

"Seems like it. This entire thing has turned into a massive shit storm."

He waited for Frankie to chastise his language, but she said nothing. She turned on the seat heaters and cranked up the temperature in the car.

CHAPTER 57

WHEN THEY WALKED INTO THE POLICE STATION, THERE WAS AN unmistakable sense of nervousness and fear. All eyes turned toward them. Curtis took a stand at the front of the station, trying to look as authoritative as possible. Frankie walked around the outside of the room to Dr. Novak and began speaking with her.

"Everyone," said Curtis to the assembled police officers, "I know some terrible things have happened, but we can't do anything about it. We need to look forward. The first thing we have to do is stop Robert Randall from getting out of Blind River. Are the roadblocks up?"

"Yes," replied a sergeant.

"What about news reports about rewards?"

"It's on every local channel and the channels of adjacent towns."

"Good. Any bites yet?"

"Not yet, sir."

Curtis nodded and looked up at the ceiling, trying to think of where Robert would go. His thoughts were interrupted when his phone rang. He fished it out of his pocket and answered, turning away from the assembled crowd.

"Hello?"

"Hey," said Monica. "Trevor's here at the hospital with Kendra. He told me what happened. Are you okay?"

"I'm fine. How are things there?"

"Chaotic, actually. The doctors are having a tough time keeping everyone calm."

"How are things going with Dad?" Curtis didn't want to think about his father, but if he didn't ask the question, it would bug him. Everything that had happened over the past few days had reminded him how fragile life could be.

"As good as you could expect. Father Bryan dropped by to help with the funeral stuff."

Monica didn't offer any more information, and Curtis didn't ask. It was enough that she was taking care of it. He would wait to tell her about Josh. They ended the call without saying goodbye.

A landline rang, and one of the cops picked it up. He spoke with the caller for a few moments, then hung up. He looked up at Curtis and shook his head.

Curtis sighed and started pacing. They were waiting for something to break free and show them where Robert had gone.

Someone must have seen him.

CHAPTER 58

ROBERT TOOK A LEFT TURN TOWARD THE HIGHWAY AND WAS greeted by a long line of cars. In the distance, he could see a police roadblock checking everyone moving through.

It seemed as though everyone in Blind River was trying to evacuate, probably as a response to the shootout and killings at the police station, along with Marino's escape.

Robert cursed under his breath.

As he drove past the row of cars, he smiled. No one was looking at him.

Something in the corner of his eye drew his attention, and he jerked his head to the right. On a porch to his right stood a middle-aged woman with streaks of gray in her hair. Her young daughter was pointing directly at him, and the woman's eyes had gone wide. She grabbed her daughter's shoulder and pushed her inside, her eyes constantly darting back to Robert.

Robert cursed again and accelerated, trying to think of a way out of Blind River that might not have occurred to the authorities. He heard more pounding from the trunk as Natasha tried to get his attention.

She would understand eventually.

Suddenly, an idea occurred to him.

He turned right and pushed the gas pedal to the floor, the forest looming in the distance.

That was how it had to end. It would be poetic.

CHAPTER 59

"WE'VE GOT HIM," SHOUTED ONE OF THE OFFICERS, PUTTING down the phone. "East side. Highway entrance. Woman reports that she saw Robert Randall drive past the blockade and turn back toward town."

"We're on it," said Curtis, grabbing his coat off the back of his chair. Frankie was already ready to go. He walked to the officer and took the notepad page with the woman's address. "Keep us updated."

Curtis and Frankie left the station and climbed into their car. Curtis looked up at the sky and felt baffled that it wasn't even four in the afternoon.

As they climbed into the car, Frankie looked at Curtis. "Are you okay?"

"What do you mean?" he said.

"Your dad, Marino and all that's happened. Are you okay?"

"Is this you or Johnson asking?"

"It's me, Curtis. You're my partner. Be honest with me."

"I'll be fine once we get that sociopathic sack of shit Robert Randall. Let's go."

Frankie nodded, turning on the car's engine.

When they rang the doorbell at the woman's house, the door opened slowly, the chain still across. She asked to see their identification before opening the door all the way. She introduced herself and her daughter, then explained what she'd seen. She was absolutely certain it was Robert Randall.

They thanked her and exchanged contact info before returning to the car.

"Okay," said Frankie as they pulled out of the driveway. "If he came this way, where would he be going?"

"He'd be trying to find any streets not blocked off. I'll check." Curtis spent a minute on the phone talking to the dispatcher and was told with absolute certainty there were no roads exiting Blind River that weren't being monitored. Assuming the witness got her time right, Robert Randall had still been within the town limits when the last of the roadblocks had been set up.

"Okay," said Curtis after hanging up. "If he wasn't able to get out of town, where would he go?"

"He couldn't go home," said Frankie.

"He couldn't go to any of his friends' houses."

"Unless they think he's innocent. There's a reason he was never suspected until it became obvious."

"It could be someone he worked with in the Marino era. I'll check known associates."

Curtis took out his phone again and called the station. While he was on the line, Frankie drove on a circuit of the town. They checked the roadblocks and the lines of cars being held up while the cops checked everyone's identification and made sure they weren't trying to smuggle anyone out.

Curtis frowned. He hung up and said, "Turn left here."

They turned toward the forest and the road where they had first gone when they arrived in Blind River. Curtis instructed Frankie to pull into the same parking lot as that first afternoon where he'd told her about Sam Marino.

There was a single car parked at the edge of the forest.

"Is that what I think it is?" said Frankie as she parked.

"That's Robert's car." Curtis couldn't prove what he said next, but he somehow knew it was true. "He's going to take Natasha into the forest," he said. "He's going to kill her, and dump her body into the Blind River. Then he'll do the same to himself."

CHAPTER 60

NATASHA OPENED HER EYES, HER HEAD POUNDING, AND LOOKED up at the canopy of trees above her. The sun was shining through. It took her a moment to realize where she was.

She remembered the trunk opening. She'd been ready to jump out in anger, but Robert had been ready. The butt end of a shotgun had hit her in the face. She could taste blood.

She slowly became aware of being dragged, her arms above her head and her legs dragging through the muddy leaves on the forest floor. She tried to extract her arms from Robert's firm grip, but he seemed to not even notice.

"Robert," she said, flailing her legs against the muddy ground, unable to get any traction. "What are you doing? Robert!"

"Don't scream," he said calmly. "You'll ruin it."

"Ruin what?"

"Since I first saw you, Natasha, I knew you were special. You understood me. For that, I want to give you something no one else can."

"What?"

"You, my last love, will be my last victim, as my first love was my first."

Natasha frowned in confusion. She thought about Robert's wife, about how she'd gone to Florida for an experimental cancer treatment and never come back, how she'd been buried in South Carolina with her ancestors. The story had never been questioned. It had seemed wrong to question a grieving husband and a valued member of the community about his dead spouse. She thought of the fourth body in the river, the most desecrated of the four. She knew Robert hadn't killed Miranda O'Connell, but hadn't gotten the chance to ask who the fourth body was.

Now she knew.

Natasha took a few moments before it truly dawned on her that she was going to die. This wasn't how she wanted to go out. She had too much left to write and tell the world.

She took a deep breath and screamed at the top of her lungs. Her voice echoed through the trees. Birds flew from the branches.

"We're too far into the forest," said Robert. "No one can hear you."

Natasha gathered all her strength and screamed again.

Robert sighed.

CHAPTER 61

STANDING AT THE EDGE OF THE FOREST, CURTIS FROWNED AS birds flew from the top of the trees.

"There's blood in the trunk," said Frankie, walking up to him. "I've called it in. If Robert went in there, we're too late. He could be anywhere."

"He's going to the Blind River."

"That pond, you mean?" said Frankie. "The sinkhole? Where he hid the girls?"

"Yeah, Jeff and I used to joke that the pond was the true Blind River the town was named after."

Frankie nodded, although she obviously thought it was a stupid name for a pond.

Curtis unholstered his gun. "The cops won't get here in time. I'm going in."

"Are you serious?"

"Someone has to save Natasha. No matter what she did, she deserves better than this."

"I'm coming with you."

Curtis turned back to Frankie. "No, stay here and meet the cops."

"If you think I'm letting you go in after that maniac without backup, you're insane."

"There's no talking you out of this, is there?"

"There is not."

Curtis sighed. "Fine, let's go."

CHAPTER 62

THEY STOPPED.

Natasha looked up at the trees, trying to figure out where they were. Robert let go of her arms, and she fell to the ground, her head landing in the mud.

"Isn't it beautiful?" said Robert. "I've always loved this pond. Curtis Mackley told me about it. It almost makes you believe magic could exist, don't you think?"

Natasha rolled over and looked at where Robert pointed.

She recognized the pond from the pictures. Only a few pieces of crime scene tape remained. At another time, she might have agreed it was beautiful. Now it was a thing of horror, of death and suffering. If she went into that pond, she'd never come out.

She had to move, but her body wouldn't listen.

She had to get out of there. She managed to get onto her knees. She had one foot in front of her when she was yanked backward by her hair. She yelped in pain as she fell back onto the ground.

"You're not going anywhere," said Robert. "Not until we're done."

CHAPTER 63

CURTIS SPRINTED THROUGH THE FOREST, FRANKIE JUST BEHIND him. Normally, Frankie would be outpacing him, but Curtis remembered the terrain from his childhood. He maneuvered through the trees and sweated as the oppressive sun beat down on him.

There was a scream, straight ahead. It was faint but undeniably female. It was in the direction of the Blind River.

Curtis found another reserve of energy he didn't know he had and accelerated his pace. Leaves crunched behind him as Frankie did the same.

As they ran, the screaming got louder.

"Leave her alone!" shouted Curtis as he burst into the small clearing around the pond, pulling out his gun.

He aimed at the broad back of Robert Randall. Natasha was on her stomach, her head and neck over the edge of the pond, a shotgun pressed into her neck.

"Curtis," said Robert, turning his head to look at them. "How nice of you to come."

Robert looked completely calm.

Frankie emerged from the forest beside Curtis, her gun pointed at Robert.

"No one else needs to get hurt, Robert," said Frankie. "Let her go."

Robert laughed. "What are you going to do? Shoot me? So what? I'll take death over being in a prison cell any day of the week. I've killed many people, Curtis. I've been blessed with the chances that have been bestowed upon me."

"You're insane," said Curtis.

"I knew you wouldn't understand. Now, if you'll excuse me." Robert turned and put a second hand on the shotgun, pushing Natasha's face toward the water.

Curtis fired three times, all three bullets hitting the broad target of Robert's back.

Frankie added another four, making Robert's back a mosaic of bloody fabric. Robert stumbled forward, his foot slipping on the edge of the pond. He pulled the trigger of the shotgun and blew a hole in a nearby tree. With his arms flailing in a last-ditch effort to steady himself, he pitched forward into the Blind River.

He hit the water, and a small tidal wave spread out from his body, splashing against the edges of the pond. The waves continued for a few moments as he sank below the surface, the water turning a bright red. He disappeared into the darkness, where his body would be absorbed by the sand, just as four of his victims had been.

Natasha lurched back from the rapidly bloodying water and gasped, spinning around to a sitting position. Frankie ran up and put her arms around Natasha, trying to stop her shaking.

Natasha just kept muttering, "I'm sorry. I knew it was him. I should have stopped him. I'm sorry. I'm sorry."

Frankie held her close, reassuring her it would all be okay.

Curtis stepped to the edge of the pond. He looked down through the bloodied water. He pointed his gun into the pond, looking for something to shoot. Somehow, it didn't seem that farfetched that Robert would emerge from the pond.

After a few moments, seeing nothing, Curtis holstered his gun.

He stepped back from the pond and its murky depths into which the killer had fallen. He hoped he'd never have another reason to come back here.

CHAPTER 64

Here Lies
Police Chief Gordon Mackley
Father of Josh, Curtis, and Monica
Husband of Barbara
Protector of Blind River
July 7th, 1943-April 17th, 2017

CURTIS STARED at the tombstone and sighed. He was standing to one side of the grave. The graveyard had been a community gathering place on that day.

Father Bryan looked exhausted as he went back and forth between the church and the graveyard for the endless funerals.

Gordon Mackley's funeral had been first, as it had been the first organized. The turnout had been far greater than Curtis could ever have imagined.

Many of the attendees had been former supporters of a

return to Marino control. After the events of the last few days, maybe they saw that Chief Mackley had made Blind River the best it could be.

Sam Marino had been transported to a maximum-security prison in Florida, where he would be stripped of the liberties he had earned over years of good behavior at Blind River Penitentiary.

Robert Randall's body had been pulled from the Blind River in the early hours of that morning, despite Curtis's protests that the appropriate punishment would be for his body to rot at the bottom of the pond. The FBI had taken his body wherever they take bodies no one wants to claim.

Natasha Nolowinski had been fired from her position at the Blind River Observer, but she hadn't been charged with anything.

She was claiming to be a victim and nothing more. She claimed her apologies had never happened, that Curtis and Frankie were making up a story. Along with the still-missing notepad, it was looking like Natasha would walk free. Frankie had already gone back to Manhattan to give their side of the story to Johnson.

"It's weird, isn't it?" said a voice.

Curtis looked up. Monica was standing beside him. He looked back at the grave. He'd told Monica about what had happened to Josh.

"Where's Trevor?" he said.

"He headed back to the station," said Monica. "There's some talk about him becoming the new chief. Tucker always wanted it to be him."

Curtis smiled as a memory of Trevor came into his head. "Trevor was the guy in high school who got the shit kicked out of him by the hockey captain, right? He was being too cocky as a freshman."

Monica laughed. "Yeah, that was him. He'll be glad to know you finally remembered him."

"I remember him. Always felt bad for him."

"He doesn't like talking about it."

"Trevor would make a great chief."

"He was always Tucker's favorite."

Curtis sighed. "How was Nate's funeral?"

A breeze swept through the graveyard.

Monica sighed and looked around the full graveyard. Everyone knew someone who had a funeral that day. Among the dead were two police chiefs, two police officers, one FBI agent, one father, and the three murdered girls.

"I was only married to him for six months," said Monica, "but I felt like I knew him. Listening to the people who really knew him talk about him makes me think twice. It seems like they remember a different person than I do."

"Maybe they just remember the best parts."

"Maybe." Monica glanced at him. "Can I ask you something?"

"Sure."

"What happened with Amber?"

Curtis looked over the tombstones. "I loved her, but I couldn't stay with her."

"What happened?"

Curtis took a deep breath. "It all started when she got pregnant."

Monica raised an eyebrow. "Did she have the kid?"

He nodded.

"And you just left?"

"No," said Curtis. "I found out it wasn't mine."

Monica turned and looked at him. She seemed like she was trying to find the right words. Finally, she said, "Amber cheated on you?"

Curtis nodded. "She came clean about a month after the baby was born. She wanted me to stay and raise it as though it was my own. She tried to tell me she'd made a mistake, and it would never happen again. She said she wouldn't be able to support herself as a single mother."

Monica sighed. "You didn't believe her?"

Curtis shrugged. "How could I? She had lied about a kid I'd been treating as my own for a month. So the next day, I left and enrolled in the FBI. I haven't seen her since. I had to make a choice, and I chose the FBI."

"Curtis," said Monica. "I don't know what to say."

Curtis put his hands into his pockets. "I send her money every month. Just in case she doesn't have enough for the kid."

Monica nodded. "Does Melanie know?"

"Yeah," said Curtis, "and it makes her nervous. She thinks it means I'll be a bad dad, that when something goes south, I'll just run away."

Monica put a hand on his shoulder. "It doesn't mean that at all."

Curtis nodded. "Thanks."

They stood like that for a few minutes, the closest they'd been to one another in a decade.

Monica sighed. She took a slip of paper from her pocket and handed it to Curtis.

He unfolded it. Written on the slip was the name of a restaurant. He looked up at Monica.

"Miranda O'Connell," she said. "Drop by on your way back to Manhattan." She sighed. "It was good seeing you, Curtis. Maybe next time you come back to Blind River, it'll be under better circumstances."

Monica removed her hand, turned, and walked away, leaving Curtis alone at their father's grave.

Curtis stared at the words written there, wondering how anyone could think a few lines could encapsulate a life.

CHAPTER 65

CURTIS PULLED OFF THE HIGHWAY INTO THE DINER'S PARKING lot.

He parked the rental car and walked inside. Men in plaid shirts leaned over the counter, chowing down on bacon and eggs and drinking coffee. They looked up when Curtis entered and took a seat at the counter, eyeing his nice but wrinkled suit for a moment before returning to their meals.

Curtis took a long sip when the waitress brought him coffee. "Thanks. Some oatmeal with brown sugar, please."

"You got it." The server retreated down the counter to deal with someone else. Curtis sipped the weak coffee and gazed into the kitchen, trying to find her.

After a few moments, a young girl holding a large bag of uncooked fries walked by and dumped the bag into the deep fryer.

Curtis took a moment before he realized he was staring. He managed to look casual before Miranda O'Connell met his gaze, giving him a questioning glance before returning to work.

Curtis kept an eye on her while he ate his oatmeal and paid his bill. He walked out of the restaurant and moved his car to a spot where he could see all the exits.

Almost two hours later, Miranda O'Connell exited the back door of the restaurant. She walked toward a bike locked to a chain link fence.

Curtis exited the car and walked toward her.

"Miranda," he said as he approached.

She froze, then tried to pretend she hadn't heard him, continuing to unlock her bike from the fence.

"Miranda O'Connell," he said. "I have something of yours."

She turned toward him, her hands still on the bike lock. Her eyes opened wide when she saw the dirty, blood-covered butterfly hairclip in Curtis's hand.

"Who are you?" she said.

"FBI Special Agent Curtis Mackley. I'm not here to arrest you or to take you anywhere, if that's what you're thinking."

"Prove it," said Miranda.

Curtis took out his identification and threw it to her. She caught it, read it, and nodded before chucking it back.

"I heard you caught the killer." Miranda crossed her arms. "We did."

"So what am I? A loose end?"

Curtis shrugged. "You can call it that if you want."

Miranda looked at the diner. "What do I need to say to make you leave?"

"Tell me why you faked your kidnapping."

Miranda shrugged. "I couldn't take it. The pressure from my parents was unbearable. I just wanted to be a teenager, have fun, hang out with my friends. My parents wanted me to study and boost my college resume all day every day."

"Surely they didn't want to destroy your social life."

"I didn't have friends." Miranda looked away. "Not one. My parents were convinced family was all I needed, and that success was all that mattered. It was about how it reflected on them. It was nothing to do with me. I've had more fun and made more friends in the weeks since I ran away than I have in my entire life. Isn't that what life is about? Making relationships that matter?"

Curtis fingered the butterfly hairclip. "Your parents deserve to know. They love you."

Miranda shrugged. "You can tell them. I'm not going back. I turned eighteen. You can't make me."

Curtis was about to speak, but there was something in Miranda's voice that seemed final.

Curtis smiled. "If you say so."

He tossed Miranda the hairclip, then held out his contact card. "If you ever need anything, give me a call."

Miranda walked up to him tentatively, grabbed the card, then retreated. "Thank you."

Curtis nodded, turned on his heel, and walked back to his car, without looking at Miranda.

He shot her one last glance in the rearview mirror as he drove away.

Curtis knew he'd done the right thing. There was something about Miranda that had been missing from all those family photos Curtis had seen. She looked happy.

It was the same smile Amber had when she told him she was pregnant.

Curtis pulled over to the side of the road, sweat beading on his forehead. He'd driven less than a mile.

He grabbed his phone and dialed Frankie.

She answered on the third ring. "This is Lassiter."

"Frankie, it's me."

"Curtis," said Frankie. "How are you doing? How was the funeral?"

"It was fine. How are things there?"

"Johnson believed my version of events."

"That's good."

"Was there anything else?"

"What do you mean?"

"Was there another reason you called?" said Frankie.

"Yes, there was." Curtis was silent for a long moment. "I need you to do something for me."

"What?"

"I need you to go on the FBI database and look up Amber Henderson, born March 16th, 1985."

"What's this about, Curtis?"

"It's about her son. I had the option to raise him and chose to join the FBI instead."

There was a long silence. "I'll check," said Frankie.

The call ended. Curtis turned on the air conditioning. He pulled back onto the road and headed for home, feeling more confident about his future than he had in a long time.

For the duration of the drive back, all he could think about was Amber's child and the child he would have with Melanie, who was due to give birth in five months.

When he got home, he parked on the side of the road. He turned off the car and sat there for a few moments. There were lights on inside. He could see Melanie moving around inside, probably wondering when Curtis would be back, or if he would leave her like he did to Amber.

"I came back," he said, stepping out of the car and walking toward the house. "Just like I promised."

ALSO BY BEN FOLLOWS

My other books are all available on Amazon in Ebook, Print, and Kindle Unlimited.

The Absence of Screams

The Compound

The Other Side of Goodbye

ACKNOWLEDGMENTS

Thank you to all my beta-readers for their advice and critiques.

Thank you to Michael Garett from manuscriptcritique.com and to James Osborne for editing this book.

Thank you to James at GoOnWrite.com for the cover design.

ABOUT THE AUTHOR

Ben Follows graduated from McGill University with a degree in history and economics. He lives in the Greater Toronto Area.

For More Information:
BenFollows.com
BenFollowsbooks@gmail.com

41537469R00182

Made in the USA
Middletown, DE
07 April 2019